WINTERHAVEN

Annabel Tyler's boss sent her to the Scottish Highlands to save Winterhaven, the estate of a valued client. But at every turn Annie found a mystery to unravel. Who was David O'Neal, the stranger who seemed to know all about her? What was the dark secret of Winterhaven's deep loch? And were the estate and its inhabitants cursed? But then Annie fell in love with the new master of Winterhaven — and things took an even more dramatic turn!

JANET WHITEHEAD

WINTERHAVEN

Complete and Unabridged

LINFORD
Leicester

First published in Great Britain in 2007

First Linford Edition
published 2008

Names, characters and incidents in this book are
fictional, and any resemblance to actual events,
locales, organisations, or persons living or dead is
purely coincidental.

British Library CIP Data

Whitehead, Janet
  Winterhaven.—Large print ed.—
Linford romance library
1. Highlands (Scotland)—Fiction
2. Love stories 3. Large type books
I. Title
823.9'14 [F]

ISBN 978–1–84782–074–7

Published by
F. A. Thorpe (Publishing)
Anstey, Leicestershire

Set by Words & Graphics Ltd.
Anstey, Leicestershire
Printed and bound in Great Britain by
T. J. International Ltd., Padstow, Cornwall

**For Angelia Collins,
Who did all the hard work!
Thanks, Angie!**

1

It was just coming up to five o'clock on a murky Friday afternoon when Clive Porter poked his head around the office door and said, 'Annie — could I have a quick word?'

Pausing in the act of filing some documents away before getting ready to go home, Annabel Tyler could barely hide her disappointment. It had been just one in a series of long, demanding weeks, and she had been promising herself a stress-free weekend during which she might unwind. Now, however, it looked as if she was going to be denied the early start she'd been hoping for.

'Won't take a minute,' he added persuasively.

'All right,' she replied with a smile.

As Mr Porter disappeared, Annabel — Annie, as she preferred to be known to her friends and colleagues — set down her work and glanced across at Kim Hill, a nineteen year-old blonde girl who acted as a combination switchboard operator and typist for the firm. 'If I don't see you before you go,' she said, 'have a nice weekend.'

'And you, Annie.'

Annie left the office and went through to Mr Porter's inner sanctum. It was much like the room she had just left behind her; square, remarkably orderly, with clearly labelled filing cabinets and shelves filled with law books. But the firm had not always been so well organised; Annie had in large part been responsible for the transformation.

The room was dominated by Clive Porter's large mahogany desk, at the centre of which lay a green oblong blotter, and upon which now rested a folder stamped with the firm's familiar logo — PORTER, SIMS AND JOHNSON, SOLICITORS. 'Come in, Annie,' invited Porter. 'Take a seat. I'll try not to keep you a moment.'

She took the visitor's chair, so that they could sit directly opposite each other across the desk. The office smelled of rose-scented furniture polish, and spider-plants draped their pale green fronds over the rims of their pots on the window-sill. The room was cool, for this was late October, and relatively peaceful. The electric wall-clock hummed softly. Outside, a phone rang. The sounds of crawling traffic just beyond the closed window in Chancery Lane were muted but for the occasional angry hoot of a horn.

Clive Porter opened the file and scanned it briefly. He was in his late forties, with a pale face, very dark brown eyes and oiled black hair. After a moment he looked up to regard the girl sitting across from him. Annie was twenty four years old, quite tall and slim, with short black hair and hazel eyes. She had naturally tanned skin, a small nose and heart-shaped lips. Dressed in a smart black skirt and matching jacket over a startlingly-white blouse, she appeared every inch the office administrator that she was.

'Let me ask you something,' he said at length. 'How long have you been with us now?'

She considered. 'About a year.'

'And do you think you've learned anything of value in that time?'

Again she smiled. She knew that Clive Porter always led up to a specific subject by means of a very circuitous route, and that it was always as well to humour him, for though he was a quiet and almost shy man away from his work, he could out-perform the most experienced Thespian in the court-room. Annie had seen that much herself, whilst assisting him over the last few months, and at first she had been surprised that the black-garbed orator arguing points of law so confidently in court could be the same basically sweet-natured and retiring man she knew at the office.

'I'd like to think I've learned my fair share,' she answered after a while. And so she had, for when she was not dealing with the day-to-day running of the office, it was her job to research information on behalf of the three partners, and prepare and organise their caseloads for them. When a new action came up, she undertook practically all the preliminary groundwork for the solicitors, leaving them free to concentrate on more important matters, and it was a job she did thoroughly and well.

'I have a very tricky case in the pipeline,' Porter explained. 'There's no money in it for us; I'm doing it more as a favour. One last, personal favour, you might say. But that doesn't mean it's not of any great importance. It is. In fact, unless it's handled properly, it could spell the end of everything our client — our late, lamented client — ever worked for.' He looked directly into her face, waiting to see her reaction. 'Do you think I could trust *you* to handle it properly?'

Caution made her pause before replying. If the job was as important as

Mr Porter made it sound, then perhaps he should employ someone more qualified for the task. But then again, she had proven her worth more than once over the past year or so. Mr Porter would not have involved her if he didn't have confidence in her abilities.

'I . . . I would do my best,' she replied honestly. 'But perhaps you'd better tell me exactly what it's all about before I commit myself. I wouldn't want to let you down.'

He nodded. 'Yes, perhaps I should.' His sigh was expressive as he tried to organise everything in his mind. 'Well, I said this was tricky, and so it is. Are you familiar with the Logan file?'

'Not really.'

'We've represented the Logans of Cairn Cawdor for a number of years now. They are not exactly rich, but they are — or were, at least — comfortably off, and once owned a sizeable part of the countryside around the family estate, Winterhaven, which is in the northwest of Scotland.

'We never had to do much for old Andrew Logan — the laird of the manor, if you will — but for all of that he was a valued client, since he referred a number of lucrative contracts our way over the years. But poor Andrew met with an accident about a fortnight ago — he drowned in the lake on the estate, though I'm at a loss as to why a seventy eight year-old man whose health was questionable in the first place should decide to go fishing on a grey Scottish loch at such an unseasonable time of year. Anyway, there is no doubt that Andrew's death is a tragedy. But it has brought to light some serious financial problems for Winterhaven, problems Andrew had hitherto kept well hidden, and until they are resolved, we cannot proceed with the reading of his will.'

Annie digested that, then asked, 'What exactly is the nature of these 'financial problems'?'

'Put simply, I suspect the old man lost his head for business a few years ago, and instead of asking for help, just

7

allowed the situation to go from bad to worse. He ran up debts, failed to make the most of his assets — you know the kind of thing.' He shrugged. 'Basically, I don't think he wanted to admit that he was growing older and perhaps losing his grip a little. I knew him, of course. He was a fine old gentleman. But . . . '

He let the sentence hang.

'But fine old gentleman or not,' he went on, 'Andrew Logan has left his heirs in a bit of a pickle. His debts are quite staggering, and his creditors are many. Something has got to be sorted out, these people paid off, the estate's legal affairs put back into order. I feel I owe him that, at least.

'That's where *you* come in. I need someone to go up and take a look around the place, see if there's anything we can use at Winterhaven to pay off all of Andrew's debts and clear the slate before his grandson takes over.'

'Grandson?'

'Yes. Andrew only had one living relative, a grandson of whom he was always very fond.'

Clive Porter's face grew troubled, and his manner was somewhat distracted.

'Mr Porter . . . ' Annie began uncertainly.

'Yes?'

'Is there — something *more* — to all of this?'

He smiled sadly. 'Yes, there is,' he confessed. 'Andrew helped us once. About twenty years ago. The practice was going through a bad patch. For a while it looked as if we might have to shut up shop altogether. Andrew got to hear of it somehow, got on a train and came down to see us. He was a force to be reckoned with in those days, so vibrant. It was quite a turn-up — a client coming to see us in order to *give* advice, not *request* it.' He closed the folder with an air of finality. 'Well, to cut a long story short, he must have liked what he saw, three young — well, young*ish* — men full of ambition, and he advanced us enough capital to 'weather the storm', as it were. We never forgot him for that, and nothing gave me greater pleasure than eventually justifying the faith he had in us.

'That's why I said that this business was more in the nature of a favour than anything else. I want us to clear those debts, get the Logan finances back on the right track, and I want you to go and evaluate the situation first-hand in order to see exactly how we can do it.'

He gave her a searching look. It was, as he well knew, an awesome responsibility. 'I can give it to someone else if you think it might be too big for you,' he said, holding up the folder.

For a moment she was lost in thought, sifting the implications. 'Oh, no. I'll handle it. But it's a big job, as you say. I just hope I don't let you down.'

'I think you have more ability than you give yourself credit for, Annie,' he said, passing the folder across to her. 'I imagine you'll need to spend about a week up in Scotland if you're to do the job properly. Does that present any problems?'

'No. I have my own flat, as I think you know, and I live alone.'

'Right, then. The folder contains all the background information you're likely to want to know. How do you want to go up to Scotland?'

'By train,' she said.

He nodded. 'Yes, it's a devil of a journey by car, and I'm not so sure you'd get a flight at such short notice.' He thought briefly, then said, 'Tell you what. I'll get your ticket and drop it in to you over the weekend, if that's okay. That way you can get an early start first thing on Monday morning. You can fix up your accommodation when you get to Cairn Cawdor. The village is about six miles from the house, and as memory serves, it has a nice little hotel.' He smiled at her. 'Good luck, Annie. I have every confidence in you.'

Annie took the folder and stood up. 'Thank you, Mr Porter,' she replied.

She went back into the outer office.

11

She was all alone now; Kim had already gone home. She stared at the folder. Upon it had been stencilled the name LOGAN, ANDREW, and beneath that, WINTERHAVEN. With her hazel eyes, she traced the name of the estate she had been empowered to try and save, and knew a moment of apprehension. Winterhaven. Winterhaven. It had a strange ring to it, a sound that was at once both appealing and somehow *bleak*.

She wondered what awaited her in that remote, far-off location, but of course, simply had no idea. And little did she know that it was destined to be something so completely fantastic that not even her wildest flight of fantasy could prepare her for the strange experiences that lay ahead.

She glanced down at her wristwatch. It was nearly a quarter to six. Time she embarked upon the journey home to her modest little flat in Snaresbrook, though she doubted now that her weekend was going to be as stress-free as she had hoped. Oh well . . .

She reached for her coat and shrugged into it, then gathered her bag and the folder together and switched off all the lights before leaving.

★ ★ ★

Annie had deliberately kept the weekend free in order to spend some quiet hours catching up on her reading and generally lazing around. Whilst there would be no time for lazing around now, however the Logan file certainly ensured that there was plenty for her to read and absorb.

Halfway through Saturday afternoon, she received a phone-call from Mr Porter. He had purchased her train ticket and wondered if it would be all right to drop it over later that afternoon. She told him that it would be fine. When he arrived, she found that the open-ended return ticket would take her all the way from Euston Station to Glasgow Central via the

Inter-City service, and bring her back at any time within the next fortnight. From Glasgow, she could either catch one of the many picturesque connecting services that would take her further north and west to Cairn Cawdor, or hire a car. Before he left, the solicitor also gave her two hundred pounds to cover her various expenses.

Annie spent Sunday afternoon packing for the trip. She also telephoned her parents, to tell them that she was going to Scotland for a week or so, on business. Monday morning came around quickly, and it was with butterflies in her tummy that she finally travelled into central London to catch the one-two-five up to Glasgow.

The station was all dash and scurry by the time she arrived, hefting a suitcase in one hand and a flight bag over her shoulder, but the organised chaos she had expected to find at the mainline station had been intensified due to a fault with the mechanical notice boards. None of the would-be travellers seemed to know which platforms they should go to in order to find their trains. Neither could they decipher the somewhat-garbled Tannoy announcements echoing around the great station, and Annie was no exception.

Always thorough, she had allowed herself ample time to find her train, but in all the confusion, that time swiftly began to tick away. She battled through the crowds, wishing that she hadn't packed quite so much luggage for the trip, until at last she found a beleaguered railway official and asked him which platform she should go to in order to board the Glasgow train. When he told her, she realised with some dismay that she was on the far side of the station to where she should be, and that it was going to take her twice as long to wade through so many frustrated passengers as it would have had things been running more smoothly.

Still, she told herself, she must not panic as she struggled towards her destination. With any luck, her train's departure would be delayed for some reason. She told herself wryly that she was probably the only person there at Euston who was actually *hoping* for a delay of some sort!

She continued to fight her way across the busy concourse, uncomfortably aware all the while that every clock she passed showed that time was being eaten up at an alarming rate. From somewhere up ahead she heard a shrill whistle. Was that the signal for her own train to move off, or had it come from a different platform? She felt heat rush to her face and was certain that she must be turning bright red.

A porter pushing a trolley stacked with newspapers appeared in her path and would not deviate from it, forcing her to make the detour around him. Again she wished fervently that she had refrained from packing so much luggage. After all, she was only expecting to be away for a week, if that!

At last her platform came into sight and she heaved a sigh of relief. Nearly there, thank goodness.

Then the strap on her flight bag broke.

At first she wasn't quite sure what had happened. Then, as the bag slapped hard against the stone flooring, realisation set in.

Another whistle blew. She was going to miss her train. She *knew* she was. So near, she thought, and yet so far! And there was a three-hour delay before the next one.

She came to a halt, turned and bent to retrieve her fallen bag. As she scooped it up, the little wallet holding her expense money and ticket slipped from the breast pocket of her jacket, along with some loose change she had been keeping handy in case she needed to use a public telephone.

'Oh . . . '

She watched the coins land with a musical tinkle, then bounce and roll in every direction. Again she heard a whistle blow, and its sound sent a thrill of urgency through her. It was followed by a few shouts she could not understand, and then the slamming of several train doors.

Her spirits dropped. It was not the best way she could have hoped to start this most important and challenging assignment, by missing her train.

Desperately she endeavoured to gather up her luggage, wallet and small change, but panic made her fingers unco-operative and clumsy. It was then, in that moment of utter confusion and despair, that a shadow fell across her and a pleasant male voice said, 'Here — you look like you could use a hand.'

She looked up, startled. A tall man in his late twenties reached down and relieved her of her luggage, leaving her free to gather up the smaller items. She straightened up to face him a moment later, quickly running her fingers up through her short black hair and conscious that she must look a mess. 'Th-thank you,' she said.

His smile was dazzling, and as his full lips stretched wide, they revealed strong white teeth in a pristine ivory flash. He had short, curly dark-blond hair and his smooth skin was tanned a golden bronze. He was about six feet in height, which put him some six inches taller than Annie, and the body beneath his short denim jacket, white cotton polo shirt and casual, bleached jeans appeared firm and athletic. He was a startling vision, she thought, an Adonis, a knight in shining armour who had come to her rescue, and he exerted such a calming influence over her that for a moment she didn't realise that everything else, their surroundings and all the clamour that accompanied it, had simply ceased to exist.

Then, with a jolt, she realised that she was staring at him in a most impolite fashion and she blinked, forcing herself back into the real world. Flustered, she said, 'I'm sorry, I — '

'Is this your train?' he asked, indicating the sleek collection of carriages on the other side of the gate with a nod of his head.

'I . . . yes,' she replied.

'Come on, then. We'd better hurry or else we'll miss it.'

He waited for her to go through the barrier, then followed her, carrying her bags — in addition to the knapsack he wore on his back — as if they were weightless. At the far end of the platform, where autumnal sunshine streamed down onto a confused tangle of railway tracks in dusty golden bars, a porter put a whistle to his lips to indicate that the train was finally about to depart.

Annie hurried aboard the first carriage they came to and the personable young man with her luggage followed suit. He set the case and flight bag down and closed the door behind him. 'There,' he said. 'Now — do you know your seat number?'

'Oh, I can manage on my own now,' she replied. 'But thank you, anyway. I think I would have missed the train if you hadn't come along.'

He smiled. 'My pleasure.'

At that moment, the train started

forward with a jolt and Annie lost her balance, falling forward across her luggage to land against his broad chest.

He caught her easily, held her steady with big, gentle, artistic hands, and grinned down at her again. She sensed the heat coming off him through his clothes, was so close that she actually saw a few dark-blond hairs poking out from the open collar of his polo shirt. Then the train picked up speed and began to wind, serpent-like, out of the station on the first stretch of its long journey north, and gradually balance returned.

'Uh, thank you,' she said again, embarrassed not so much by the fact that she had lost balance, but because he seemed so easily to be able to exert such an unsettling influence over her.

'Don't give it another thought,' he replied. 'Now — you're *sure* I can't help you any further?'

'You've already done enough,' she told him. 'Really.'

He shrugged. 'See you, then.'

He swung his knapsack down off his back, the better to carry it along the train until he found his seat, and then, with one final nod, he left her there to watch him go.

She did exactly that for a moment, amused by the calm, confident way he had made 'See you' sound more like a prediction than a farewell. Then, with a shake of the head, she searched for her own ticket and checked which carriage and seat number she herself should head for.

She picked up her luggage and also began to work her way along the swaying carriage.

The train was crowded. She felt that it was as well that Mr Porter had booked her a seat, otherwise she might have had to make the entire five-hour journey standing up. Beyond the oblong windows an endless procession of grey-and black-brick railway buildings whispered past as the train slowly picked up speed and began to leave the inner city, bound for the northern suburbs and beyond. It was a bright if chilly day, and sunlight streamed in through the windows to puddle on the aisle floor.

Annie went through to the next carriage in the chain and began to search for her seat. Fortunately, this carriage wasn't quite so crammed. About halfway down, however, she was surprised to hear a voice say, 'I don't suppose you're looking for me by any chance, are you?' and when she looked down, she found herself once again confronted by the nameless stranger who had been such a help to her a few minutes earlier.

She smiled at him. 'I am if you're sitting in seat number four-five-seven,' she replied.

'Four-five-*six*,' he said with a flash of amusement in his sea-blue eyes. Hooking a thumb at the vacant seat beside him, he added, 'This must be yours.'

She glanced across to check. *457*. He was right. She felt his eyes on her, and once again returned her own gaze to his cleanly-crafted face. He had said they would meet again, and he had been right about that, too. But surely, it was just coincidence?

Before she could ponder it further, he climbed to his feet and relieved her of her luggage again, this time to stow it safely in the space behind their seats for the duration of the journey.

Within moments she was comfortably installed in her window seat, and he was seated beside her. All of this had happened so quickly that the speed of it had left her a little dizzy. Abruptly he extended his right hand. 'Donald,' he said by way of introduction. 'Pleased to meet you.'

She shook hands with him. His palm was smooth and warm. Once again she noticed he had long, tapering fingers, the hands of an artist, she thought.

'Annie,' she replied.

'Are you going all the way, Annie?' he asked.

Shock slackened her features. 'I beg your pardon?'

His chuckle was warm. 'Perhaps I

should rephrase that. Are you going all the way to *Glasgow*?'

She blushed slightly at her misunderstanding. 'Oh. Yes. Yes, I am, as a matter of fact.'

'Then it looks as if you've got some company — that's if you don't mind.'

'No, certainly not.'

At last the track-filled gullies wound their way through northwest London and into more open areas. Office blocks rose up, their windows filled with faceless workers, and gradually the office blocks gave way to more residential dwellings.

'I understand that we should be in Scotland some time around two o'clock,' Donald said conversationally. 'Barring signal failures, leaves on the line and the wrong kind of snow.'

She nodded, interested in this charismatic young man, though unable to say exactly why beyond the fact that he was, as she had already noted much to her consternation, extremely personable and good-looking. 'I hope you don't think I'm being personal,' she said, 'but — your accent. I can't quite place it.'

His grin was infectious. 'It's that awful mid-Atlantic twang you pick up after spending any length of time in the Colonies,' he explained.

'You've been staying in America?' she asked, intrigued.

'For about two years.'

'You must really notice a change coming back to England.'

'I have. But I can't say I was sorry to leave the States. Things didn't quite work out for me there.'

'Oh.'

She wanted to ask him what things, but that would be prying. He must have read her curiosity in her tone, though, because his next statement went some of the way towards explaining what he meant. 'I'm a writer,' he said. 'Well, a would-be writer. I wrote a couple of screenplays and an agent in Hollywood showed some interest and asked me to go over, but while it was an experience, all I did for two years was wait for the phone to ring. It never did.'

'So you came home,' she said.

'Hmmm.'

For a moment his face clouded, and again she felt a surge of curiosity about him. But then he shrugged off his melancholy and asked, 'What line are you in, anyway?'

'I'm a sort of office administrator-cum-legal assistant.'

'Sounds rather imposing.'

She smiled and ran her fingers up through her hair again. 'It isn't, I promise you. General dogsbody would be closer to the truth, but sometimes the work can be very interesting.'

'I'll bet. What takes you north of the border, then — business or pleasure?'

'Business,' she replied.

'Can you tell me anything about it?' he enquired. 'Without betraying any confidences, of course?'

She considered, glancing briefly out of the window. 'Oh, I'm certain it would seem to be a rather mundane chore by anyone else's standards, and it's certainly nowhere near as glamorous as the life you've been used to. Basically, though, I think I'm really just acting as a glorified liquidator. One of our clients died owing a lot of money recently, and regrettably I think I'm going to have to recommend that we sell off most of his holdings in order to settle his debts.'

'What a shame, to die like that.'

'Yes.'

The train rattled on along the track. Cloud bubbled up white-grey the further north they went, but occasionally sunlight managed to pierce the gauzy veil and send down its brilliant flaxen glow across ploughed fields and the odd stone-built farm building.

Annie hardly noticed the journey, however, for Donald was a born raconteur and he kept her entertained with an apparently endless flow of stories, many concerning his time in Hollywood. The book and magazine she had brought along to while away the hours lay forgotten in her bag as she listened to him in fascination, enjoying the pleasant, well-modulated tones of his voice, catching an Americanism here, a hint of Scottish brogue there, the two together forming an appealing and distinctive mixture. They broke only once for him to go to the buffet car and fetch back sandwiches and coffee. By then they were somewhere near Derbyshire, and still hurtling on at speeds well in excess of a hundred miles an hour, the russet colours of the autumn-touched countryside flying past in a blur of greens, reds, browns and yellows.

They sped into a storm shortly after that, and rain pattered and slapped against the window from out of a leaden sky. Soon the squall cleared again, though the sun was no longer able to penetrate the low cloud.

As entertaining as her companion undoubtedly was, however, Annie was not sorry when the train guard finally announced that they were approaching Glasgow Central. Late running had put them behind by more than half an hour, and although the bulk of the journey now lay behind her, she still had quite a trek ahead before she reached Cairn Cawdor.

At length, the end of the line came into sight beyond the window and as the passengers around them rose and began to collect their baggage, so Annie and her unexpected companion did likewise. After a time, the train pulled to a halt and they followed the press of other travellers onto the platform, where they stood facing each other, each oddly reserved now, with the muffled station announcements all but lost beneath innumerable other station-sounds.

She looked up into his face, not sorry to have reached their destination, but certainly sorry that the time had come to say goodbye. 'Well . . . ' she stared awkwardly. 'Thank you for being such good company, Donald. I hardly noticed the journey at all.'

'I think I probably talked too much,'

he said sheepishly. He carried her baggage to the ticket barrier, and then set it down. 'Well, Annie, take care. If I should ever need a legal assistant, you'll be at the top of my list.'

She dipped her head. 'I'm honoured.'

There was a moment of silence between them, during which they both sobered. He put out his hand again, and she took it. 'Well, goodbye, then. And good luck.'

It was with some regret that she slipped her hand out of his.

He turned and walked away across the concourse, tall, lithe, knapsack slung across his broad back. He turned once, waved, and then disappeared from sight.

Annie watched him until he was gone. She felt curiously miserable.

But *why?* She had to remind herself that she hadn't just waved her man off to war. He had been a companionable traveller, that was all; polite, interesting, *interested*, . . . but that was all. And yet his departure left her feeling somehow empty in a strange, hard-to-explain way.

With a heavy sigh, she turned her mind to other matters. How was she going to complete her journey — by rail or hire car?

The journey had left her feeling tired and slightly heavy-headed. She didn't really feel up to driving, especially since she wasn't sure how to reach her destination.

She bent, picked up her baggage and set off in search of the station's information bureau, where she was given directions on how to reach the connecting line that would take her out of the city and on to Cairn Cawdor.

2

Annie caught the West Highland steam train half an hour later, by which time the sky was already beginning to deepen with approaching evening. But the journey proved to be one long procession of beautiful scenery that even the waning light could not spoil. They wound through grassy glens, past an old, ruined castle, across a bleak moor and — most exciting of all, at least as far as Annie was concerned — across the Glenfinnian Viaduct.

She had the carriage almost to herself, and watched with interest as they passed grassy hills flecked with herds of grazing deer and sheep. With the early darkness, however, came a low mist that soon caused the train to slow down, and the remainder of the journey was made in this cautious fashion. By the time they rolled into the little stone-built station that served Cairn Cawdor, the mist had thickened to a swirling fog, and though it was only early evening, it felt more like midnight.

Annie appeared to be the only passenger to alight at the station, and when the train steamed off again, she was left all alone in the mist. She listened for a moment, but heard nothing. Presumably, such a small, out-of-the-way station was only manned part-time, and the staff had long-since gone home.

She started along the platform. The fog muted all sound and threw a shifting grey blanket across the fluorescent signs and lights overhead. She felt isolated, as if the train had mistakenly dropped her off in the middle of nowhere, but she quickly dismissed that line of thought, for it could serve no useful purpose, only increase her sense of discomfort and unease.

She left the station and stepped out onto the pavement. A car swept past, headlamps showing briefly as two yellow cones of light. She paused a moment, trying to gather her bearings. After a while, her eyes adjusted a little and she made out the blurred and somewhat indistinct lights of some shops on the far side of the road.

She listened for traffic, heard none, and crossed the narrow, sloping path. On the other side of the street she located a newsagent's shop and went inside to get directions to the hotel Mr Porter had mentioned.

Her brief conversation with the friendly newsagent made her feel less lonely, and she set off for the hotel a few moments later with a lighter heart.

From what she could see, Cairn Cawdor was built on a very slight incline. All the buildings she passed had been constructed from oddly-shaped grey-stone bricks into which had been set small, Georgian-style windows. She saw a phone box and thought briefly about letting Mr Porter know she had arrived safely. But that could wait. At the moment, she just wanted to get herself settled into a room and allow the rigors of travel to ebb out of her.

At the bottom of the road she came to a crossroads. Directly across from her, she saw the hotel's modest neon sign. The hotel itself was a long grey structure, obviously modified and enlarged over the years to accommodate a bar and restaurant as well. Now the place was almost in darkness, although amber light did show through the drawn curtains at a few windows.

The reception was small, but warm, well-lit and inviting. Doors to the restaurant and bar stood off to her left. Through them she could hear soft, relaxing music. A stout man of average height was lounging behind the desk, reading a newspaper. When he heard the front door close behind Annie, he glanced up, then straightened up and quickly set his newspaper aside. He was in his early fifties, with sandy hair, innocuous blue eyes and a ruddy complexion. His smile was broad and sincere. 'Good evenin' to ye, miss,' he said, nodding. 'Can I help ye?'

'I'd like a room, please.'

He appeared to be surprised by the request. 'For a couple o' days, is it miss?' he enquired.

'A week,' she replied. 'Possibly a bit longer.'

'Oh.'

Annie frowned. She had not thought it unusual to go to a hotel in order to obtain short-term lodgings, but for some reason, the ruddy-faced man's reaction suggested that it was. 'I'm sorry,' she said. 'Does that present a problem?'

'Well, miss . . . ' The hotelier shrugged. 'It's just that we close the hotel down for the winter the day after tomorrow.'

Now it was Annie's turn to say, 'Oh.'

'We keep the bar and restaurant open, a' course. But it's just not worth us keeping the hotel open through the winter. We just don't get the visitors.' He spread his hands. 'It *is* a bit late in the season, miss,' he added in justification of his policy. 'And we *do* open again next March.'

Annie hadn't considered the possibility of the hotel closing for the winter. Now she wondered what she was going to do for accommodation during her stay in Cairn Cawdor.

'I can billet ye up until Wednesday,' the hotelier said, breaking in on her thoughts. 'An' in the meantime, I'll put the word about, see if I can find someone who'd be willin' to rent ye a room privately, for the remainder of your stay.'

She smiled. It was, she realised dismally, as much as she could hope for. 'Thank you,' she said at length.

Apparently satisfied with the arrangement, he turned the register around to her and offered her a pen. 'Come far, miss?' he asked.

'London.'

He made a show of appearing to be impressed, because he thought she would expect it. 'On holiday, are ye?'

'No. Business.'

'Ah. Well, if it's peace an' quiet you're

lookin' for to help ye concentrate, ye've come to the right place. Cairn Cawdor has it both.'

Annie signed in and the hotelier took a key down from the board on the wall behind him. 'Here, I'll show you to your room,' he said, stepping around the desk and picking up her bags.

She followed him up a wide, polished-wood staircase that creaked underfoot. 'Will ye be wantin' an evenin' meal, Miss Tyler?' he asked over his shoulder.

'A sandwich and some tea,' she replied. 'Followed closely by an early night, I think. It's been quite a day, what with one thing or another.'

'I'll have something sent up.'

'Thank you.'

Her room turned out to be small but well-furnished and comfortable. Once she was left alone, she went into the en suite bathroom and washed her face and hands. That made her feel better, and chased away some of her heavy-headed fatigue. She waited until a young waitress had delivered her food, then rang Mr Porter at home.

It was nearly 8 o'clock and she felt tired, but not tired enough to go to sleep *just* yet. Instead she went over to the window and chewed slowly on one of her sandwiches while she stared out at the shifting fog on the other side of the glass and thought about the young man with whom she had shared her journey north, Donald. She didn't even know his surname, and yet she found herself wondering where he was now, and what he was doing.

Her reflection peered back at her like some weird, translucent phantom, but could not give her any answers.

★   ★   ★

Annie slept well and awoke early the following morning feeling refreshed and ravenous, which was surprising, for she did not usually eat in the mornings. When she went downstairs and entered the deserted dining room, however, she ordered and ate a full breakfast, wondering curiously if the clear Highland air was responsible for the sharpening of her appetite.

Her ruddy-faced host came in about half an hour later, and seeing her, hurried over. 'Ah, good mornin' to ye, Miss Tyler. Sleep well?'

'Fine thank you.'

'I haven't forgotten about your wee accommodation problem, by the way,' he assured her. 'But don't ye worry. I'm sure I can find someone who'll be happy to put you up after we close tomorrow.'

Annie thanked the man again, then asked if there was anywhere in the village where she could hire a car. He thought about it for a moment, then shook his head. 'I'm afraid not, miss. There really isn't the call for it. But old Tommy Roberts runs his own taxi service. He'd be glad to run you about, I'm sure.' He gave her a knowing wink. 'His prices are quite reasonable, too.'

Annie returned his smile. 'Where can

I find him?' she asked.

He gave her directions, and a short while later, after she had returned to her room to collect her Winterhaven dossier and don a thick blue jacket, she went in search of the taxi-driver.

The day was bright, clear and bracing. Pausing on the pavement outside, she got her first really good look at the village. It was, as she had suspected, built on a gentle slope. Now, however, she saw that it nestled against a steep, forested hill. The air tasted clear and clean. There was very little traffic, and the peace was broken only by birdsong. Everyone who passed her by had time for a smile and a greeting, even though she was a stranger.

She marvelled at her idyllic sur-roundings. It was a world apart from the busy life she had to contend with in and around central London.

Tommy Roberts lived in a charming old grey-stone house just around the corner and about half way down the street. He answered her ring at his doorbell in a baggy cardigan, loosened tie, crumpled trousers and carpet slippers. He looked big and genial, with narrow brown eyes shielded behind thick spectacles and a permanent grin on his round, jolly face. He peered at Annie for a couple of seconds, wondering if he knew her. Then, unable to place her, he said, 'Yes?'

'Mr Roberts?' she asked.

'Aye.'

'I was told that you run a taxi service. I wondered if you could take me out to Winterhaven?'

Curiosity stirred in his magnified eyes. He was doubtless wondering what business she could have out there. But all he said was, 'Och, a'course, bonnie lass. Is et noo you're plannin' on a-goin'?'

'If it's no trouble.'

'Och, a'course et's nae trouble. Hang aboot an' I'll jest get ma cap an' jacket.'

He disappeared inside and returned a few moments later wearing the garments he had mentioned. He was in his late sixties, Annie reckoned, but he was

43

remarkably sprightly for his age.

'Tis a chilly one this mornin',' he remarked as he led her across the road to an old but immaculately-kept Hillman Minx.

He unlocked the car, opened one of the rear doors for her, then settled himself behind the steering wheel. 'So — et's Winterhaven, is et?'

'Yes.'

'Aye, well, we'll have ye there in jest a mo'.'

Annie allowed herself a secret smile. Then, as Tommy Roberts started the car, gunned the engine and pulled slowly away from the kerb, she said 'May I ask you something, Mr Roberts?'

'Och, a'course ye may, wee lassie. Ask awee.'

She paused a moment, then said, 'Do you *always* talk that way?'

He made no reply right away, and for a few tummy-clenching seconds she thought she might have offended him with the question. But then he gave a hearty chuckle and said — in the loose, clipped way of the East End Cockney, 'No, love. But you know what it's like: the tourists expect it, this far north of the border.'

She laughed, too.

'Why?' he asked over his shoulder. 'Was me accent that bad? I've had no complaints before.'

'It was fine,' she replied, taking an instant liking to the man. 'But it was just a bit over the top.'

'Well, that's me all over, love,' he confessed.

He drove them along Cairn Cawdor's main street and out onto a narrow country road that was bordered by hedges, fields, trees and the occasional distant gathering of livestock.

'So,' he said conversationally. 'What takes you all the way out to Winterhaven, then?'

'Just business,' she replied vaguely, knowing better than to divulge what was, after all, a confidential matter. To change the subject, she asked, 'What brings a Cockney all the way up the Highlands?'

'Oh, this an' that,' he said, glancing at her in his rear-view mirror. 'Redundancy, mostly. Used to work down at the docks till they decided to lay us all off. I was only eighteen months away from retirement then, knew I wouldn't stand much of a chance of finding another job at that age, so I decided to set meself up as a mini-cab driver, but what with me eyesight, and all that heavy traffic in London . . . Anyway, me and the wife decided to sell out and move up here. Property's a lot cheaper, as you probably know, and the drivin's easier.'

The drive out to Winterhaven didn't take very long, and was marked by some impressive landscapes, mostly wild, wind-swept moors covered in heather, dotted with magnificent stags, stretching towards hills tufted with long grass and grey rocks, the occasional stand of trees and the odd, winding footpath.

Tall hedges obscured her view after a while, and these gradually gave way to an eight-foot high red-brick wall that followed the contours of the lane for another mile. At length Tommy rounded a wide bend in the lane and slowed the car. 'Here we are,' he said, allowing the Hillman to cruise to a halt at the mouth of a gravel drive flanked by two grand wrought-iron gates.

Annie sat forward in her seat, eager to get her first glimpse of the estate, but found her view obscured by rows of pine and larch, beyond which the drive disappeared.

'Be all right to drop you here?' Tommy asked.

'Yes, of course.'

'Will you want picking up again later?'

'Probably,' she said as she got out of the car. 'But I'm not sure exactly when. Maybe I can give you a call.'

'Right-o, sweetheart.'

'How much do I owe you?' she asked.

He told her, and she paid him.

'Look after yourself then,' he said. 'See you later.'

'Yes. 'Bye.'

She watched him turn the Hillman around, give her a wave and then drive back towards the village.

When he was no longer in sight, Annie turned back towards the estate. The chilly wind made the tree-boughs wave lazily back and forth. She set off along the gravel drive, the crunching of her footsteps mingling with the pleasant birdsong above. Rounding the curve, she saw a little thatched cottage she took to be the estate-keeper's residence.

Annie had a feeling that the cottage was empty even before she reached it, but went ahead and knocked at the front door anyway. She paused briefly, waiting for a response she didn't honestly expect to get, then chanced a quick glance through one of the little windows just to the left of the door. Immediately her suspicions were confirmed, for the room beyond the glass was virtually empty, and what few items of furniture still remained had long-since been covered with dustsheets.

This discovery put Annie in something of a quandary. She had assumed that the estate-keeper would still be in residence, and that she would be able to obtain access to Winterhaven itself through him. If, as now seemed the case, an estate-keeper was no longer employed, she would have to find some way of getting back to Cairn Cawdor in order to discover what had become of the keys.

She glanced around. It might not come to that yet, she told herself optimistically. Perhaps the estate-keeper had merely moved into the big house itself, the better to keep an eye on the property following Andrew Logan's death.

With no better option open to her, she continued on up the drive, footsteps sounding brittle and crunchy on the gravel, feeling closed in and a little claustrophobic by the trees towering skyward to either side of her. She followed the drive around another bend and came to a sudden, stunned halt, for there, at the very centre of a vast expanse of landscaped grounds perhaps a hundred yards ahead, stood the house.

Winterhaven.

It was even more impressive than she had imagined it would be, especially with the weak autumnal sunshine shafting down to bathe it in a rich golden spotlight.

The house was a mixture of styles, from Medieval to Gothic and Post Reformation. It had a roof of red tiles and an Italianate façade of smooth grey stone up and across which crept dark green ivy. The house itself was flanked by two turreted towers. Eight long, arched windows stared back at her from ground-level, four to either side of the large, ornately-carved black oaken door. Nine smaller, similar windows marked the positions of the first-floor rooms; a further nine rose up above them on the second floor.

Winterhaven was breathtakingly beautiful, although a little imposing, too. Annie stood for a time just admiring its regal lines, then shook off its entrancing spell and continued on up the drive towards the weathered stone steps that led to the front door.

Another, stronger breeze sprang up to ruffle the slightly shaggy grass stretching verdantly away to either side of her, and perhaps it was this sudden movement which gave her the feeling that someone was out there watching her. The revelation made her feel a bit uneasy, and she swiftly dismissed the idea, telling herself that she was far too level-headed to entertain such melodramatic notions, and that it was just the loneliness and atmosphere of this place that was making her feel a little strange.

In any case, perhaps she *was* being watched — but by the very man she was hoping to find, the estate-keeper.

Reaching the top step, she stretched out her right hand and worked the bell-pull. She heard the bell itself jangle somewhere deep inside the house, sounding hollow and somehow forlorn.

She waited a moment, not too hopeful of eliciting any response. She listened at the door, but heard nothing further from within. As much as she hated to admit it, it began to look more and more as if she would have to return to the village and see about tracking down the whereabouts of Winterhaven's keys.

It was just then that she heard a sharp breaking sound from around the corner of the building, and she frowned. It could, of course, be cats or — and here she shuddered — *rats*. But equally well, it could be the estate-keeper, hard at work.

'Hello?' she called. Her voice sounded somehow alien as it disturbed the stillness.

There came no reply, so she descended the steps and started off in the direction of the sound, saying again, 'Hello?'

She was halfway to the corner of the house when she heard footsteps hurry-ing — no *running* — away. That put a new thought into her head; that perhaps she had disturbed some vandals, or a burglar.

At once, and perhaps foolishly, she hurried on, hoping to catch them or at least throw a scare into them to make sure they didn't come back. By the time she reached the corner, however, there was no sign of the intruder, only the shattered remains of a stack of flower-pots someone had accidentally knocked over.

She came to a halt beside the fragments. The side of the house stretched on ahead for some forty yards, ivy climbing around the white window-frames and on towards the heights above. She looked around. About forty feet away rose up a great tangle of bushes and shrubs and trees which extended like a natural border to the property for as far as the eye could see. Late-blooming wild flowers added a cheerful splash of colour to the barrier, but the trees grew so close together that their browny-green, foresty colours threw them into gloom.

Annie peered into the woods, trying to ignore the tingling of her skin. Had something moved within that tangle? The intruder, making his escape — or deciding to come back? She strained her eyes to see, but gave up after a moment. Perhaps it had been a trick of the light, or the product of an over-excited imagination.

As she stood there, a cloud passed over the sun, and its effect was dramatic. Suddenly the entire estate was thrown into dreary grey shadow, and the air grew appreciably colder. Very gradually it began to rain, just a light, insistent drizzle at first, but almost certainly a precursor to the downpour promised by the heavy and getting-heavier clouds clustered above.

Annie shivered.

For suddenly she knew beyond all shadow of doubt that she was not alone, that she was being watched, and that she was being watched *by unfriendly eyes*.

She stood her ground there by the

brown shards of the smashed flower-pots and again tried to see into the woods. It took all her willpower not to turn and run now, for she was rapidly becoming more and more convinced that she had become the object of some sinister scrutiny. But as the clouds continued to gather overhead, so the darkness beneath the canopy of twisted, interlocked branches grew more dense, hiding whoever was in there watching her.

The wind grew a little bit stronger, making the branches and bushes shiver. The movement frightened a flock of birds foraging on the forest floor into making a sudden surge skyward.

Annie jumped at the sound of their raucous cries and flapping wings. Her heart now began to pound as logic deserted her and instinct took over. *There!* Had she glimpsed the mysterious intruder again, for just an instant? She felt sure that she had, although what with the steadily-increasing rain, she could not be sure.

Somewhere in the distance, thunder voiced its throaty rumble, adding to her sense of anxiety. The rain pattered harder against the ground. She knew she must seek shelter now, and certainly she wanted to leave this place, but she knew she dare not take her eyes away from the w —

She saw a figure coming through the woods towards her then, just as more clouds crashed together above her to make the watery air tremble.

Annie brought one hand up to her mouth and gave a short, sharp, frightened cry. She watched the figure come nearer, all shadowy, so that she could distinguish nothing save that it was the figure of a tall man, and that he was *not* a trick of the light, or the product of an over-excited imagination. He was *real*.

That he meant her some harm seemed obvious. Why else would he have fled when she had first called out to see who was there? And why else would he have hidden there in the grey twilight of the woods, watching her?

And why was he now advancing upon her?

Thunder crashed for the third time, threatening to shatter her eardrums, and all at once the cloudburst arrived in a hissing, splashing torrent.

Visibility was suddenly cut by half, and Annie lost sight of the intruder.

At once panic tightened its chilly grip on her heart and she knew that she must flee now, while she still had the chance.

She turned and ran. She wasn't sure, but she thought she heard his footfalls behind her. She slipped in her haste, cried out, somehow regained her balance and raced on, around the corner and along the front of the house, with its long, rain-washed windows watching blindly, still slipping, still believing she could hear his footsteps above the hiss of the rain, following her, *gaining* upon her —

Fear engulfed her completely, save for one small corner of her mind that remained shocked that she should lose her normal sense of control so easily.

She ran on, on, on —

Suddenly he grabbed her; that was to say, someone appeared in her *path* and grabbed her. Confusion reigned in her fevered mind. As rainwater ran like tears down her face, she began to fight him.

He held her arms firm, completely unaffected by the flurry of blows she tried to unleash against him. She heard his voice, though she could not make out what it was he was saying.

Then she heard one word.

Her name.

' . . . Annie . . . '

That went some way towards quelling her panic, though she wasn't sure why.

She fought to open her eyes wider against the lancing rain, looked up — and then she saw him.

She felt dizzy, overcome with relief, though just as confused as she had been scant seconds earlier, as she recognised him.

'*Donald!*' she cried.

And then she collapsed against the broad chest of the personable young man she'd first met the day before, at Euston Station.

3

She lost consciousness then, and the next time her eyelids twitched and fluttered open, she was stretched out on a green velvet sofa beneath one of the tall, arched windows, and the rain coursing down the outside of the panes was throwing watery shadows down across a large, cosy sitting room.

The room was quite dark, for the storm had robbed much of the light from the morning sky outside. A fire crackling cheerfully in the grate went some way to dispelling the gloom, though. Here and there sat overstuffed chairs and occasional tables. A large, gilt-framed mirror hung over the fireplace, while oil paintings of all shapes and sizes dotted the surrounding walls. The furniture, like the house itself, was old but built to last; heavy, solid and dependable.

Annie lay unmoving for a moment, still disoriented and not at all sure where she was or what had brought her here. Then the thunder gave a far-off growl and that jogged her memory. It all came back then, her trip out to Winterhaven, the man she had seen in the woods — a man she had felt certain meant her some harm.

Across the room, a voice said, 'Feeling better now?'

Annie sat up with a start and looked over at the speaker. Donald was just rising from a chair on the far side of the fire. He must have been sitting there so still and quiet that she hadn't seen him during her first baffled examination of the room.

She put a hand to her head, struggled to make sense of everything. 'Yes,' she replied after a moment. 'Yes, I feel fine. But — Donald, what on earth are *you* doing here?'

'I *live* here,' he said simply.

Surprise cleared away the last of the cobwebs in Annie's puzzled mind.

'*Live* — ?' She froze then, as everything fell into place. 'Your surname,' she said slowly and uncomfortably, 'It's Logan, isn't it?'

He nodded.

'And you grandfather . . . '

' . . . was Andrew Logan,' he said.

He came closer, so that the shadows of the rain spilling down the window spilled down him as well. He was dressed in a blue sweatshirt and jeans. The blue of the sweatshirt matched that of his bright, almost hypnotic eyes as he studied her. 'And you have come from my grandfather's solicitor,' he continued softly. 'To . . . how did you put it yesterday? Oh yes — to act as a glorified liquidator.'

Annie felt something unpleasant settle in her tummy. Obviously he must have seen and handled the folder she had brought with her from the hotel. 'I didn't mean it to sound the way it did,' she said wretchedly, but earnest in her desire to convince him of her good intentions. 'I want to do everything I can to clear your grandfather's debts and enable you to take up residence here with a clean slate.'

Something in his face relaxed slightly. 'I know,' he admitted, kneeling beside her and taking one of her hands in both of his, a gesture that sent a tingle of electricity up her arm. 'Anyway, all that's beside the point right now. Are you sure you feel okay?'

'Yes. Perfectly.'

'I'll get us some tea in a minute. And you'd better do something about drying yourself off. I took the liberty of taking your jacket off while you were unconscious, but as tempting as the prospect was, I drew the line at loosening the rest of your clothing.'

She forced a wan smile. 'My modesty remains intact, then?'

'Of course. We Logans are nothing if not chivalrous.'

'Donald,' she said.

'Hmm?'

'How long was I . . . unconscious?'

'Oh, about a quarter of an hour.

Maybe not even that.' He sobered suddenly. 'Annie — what *was* all that about just now? Outside?'

As she remembered it again, it was all she could do to repress a shudder. 'Oh, nothing.'

'Come on, now. You were out of your mind out there. It looked to me like you were running away from someone.'

'Or some*thing*,' she amended, without quite knowing why.

He frowned. 'Eh?'

She shook her head. 'Oh, I don't know,' she said with a frustrated sigh. She made a great attempt to sound casual and unconcerned as she went on, hoping to dismiss her experience as something of little importance. 'I thought I saw someone in those woods at the side of the house, and I suppose I talked myself into believing that it was a burglar or something. What with the thunder and the rain, I guess my imagination ran away with me.' She shrugged and forced a nervous, embarrassed smile. 'I lost my head, just panicked, and I ran.'

'It's a good job I caught you when I did,' he said. 'Otherwise I think you'd have run all the way back to England.' He paused for a moment, considering. 'Still, if it *wasn't* your imagination, I wonder who he was?'

'You don't have an estate-keeper, then?'

'No. Grandfather had to let him go a few months ago. There shouldn't have been anyone here except me.'

He straightened back to his full, generous height. 'I'll go get us that tea. Meanwhile, you'll find a bathroom upstairs on the first floor, third door on your left.'

'Thank you.'

He left the room silently, and she turned to look out of the window at the grey landscape beyond. Thunder growled again. But it sounded distant now, and she took some comfort from the fact that the storm was finally passing over.

But she remained puzzled. What *had*

she seen out there? Here in the warmth and comfort of the big house, she could no longer be sure. It was easier to dismiss that shadowy, advancing figure as simply a trick of the light again, and perhaps that was exactly what it was.

Feeling better, she left the room and crossed the wide hallway to climb the stairs. The house was quiet and peaceful around her. The walls were panelled with oak, sturdy and permanent. The parquet floor was covered with expensive Oriental rugs. But she was startled to find that the opulence did not extend as far as the first floor. Here the house became more derelict, with many signs of neglect and disrepair. The corridor in which she suddenly found herself was dusty and faded, a world away from the orderliness of downstairs. It smelled vaguely musty and dejected up here. Cobwebs clung to the rafters overhead, gauzy and drab.

Annie was amazed by the difference, curious too. She found the bathroom, dried herself off as best she could and returned to the sitting room downstairs as quickly as possible. Donald was waiting for her when she came back in and closed the door behind her. The rain had eased up a bit, though the sky was still overcast, and thunder still occasionally rumbled cannon-like in the far distance.

The heir to Winterhaven had fetched in a tray laden with tea-things, and was pouring from a china pot as she crossed the room and retook her seat on the sofa. She knew a moment of awkwardness in his company then — her first, for they had gotten along well the day before, and although she still found him to be eminently charming and attractive, she felt that their relationship, such as it was, had changed subtly. They were no longer merely strangers enjoying a brief and — yes, she had to confess it — a *romantic* encounter on a train; now they were business associates, and that put their relationship on an altogether more formal footing.

'Thank you,' she said as he passed her a cup.

'Sugar?'

'No, thanks.'

She stared down into the cup, seeing her own reflection mirrored in its contents. Choosing her words with care, she finally said, 'Donald — I really *didn't* mean what I said to you yesterday — about acting as a liquidator for the estate.'

'I know,' he said.

'But I want you to be absolutely sure. You're going to have to trust me in this matter, trust my judgment. Your grandfather's debts are quite staggering. But if there's any way we can settle them without having to break up the estate . . . '

'That's all I want,' he said with an unexpected depth of feeling.

She had caught sight of the Winterhaven folder on the table beside the sofa on her way back in, and now reached for it. 'Still, I think it's only fair to tell you that *something* will have to go. Your grandfather's debts weren't the kind you could hope to pay off by simply pawning the family silver. But I promise you that I will try to be as sensitive to his memory and your wishes as I can be, Donald.'

He smiled. 'I know you will,' he said. 'How is this going to work, then? You rummage around the place until you find enough old relics to put up for auction, and then we all keep our fingers crossed that we raise enough money to repay Grandfather's creditors?'

'I'm not sure yet,' she replied. 'Maybe that's the way it will turn out. Of course, it might help matters if we knew exactly why he came to run up so many debts in the first place.'

'That's easy,' he said, getting up and going over to the window, where he leaned against the frame, cup in hand, and watched the grey clouds dispersing slowly and allowing the stiff wind to blow them further north. 'Grandfather spent all his life in business. It was all he knew, really. When my grandmother died, he immersed himself in commerce all the more. But then, about fifteen years ago, he got the idea into his head that he'd spent enough years working. The time had come to enjoy his retirement. So he sold his interests and tried to live a more leisurely life. Only it didn't work out. Something happened . . . he met another woman and fell in love . . . but then *she* died as well.'

He made a sad sound in his throat and turned to look at her with half his face in shadow, the other half obscured by steam rising from his cup. Clearly he had loved his grandfather very much, and obviously found discussing the old man's life now upsetting. 'That shattered him,' he went on. 'It really did. And he was never the same afterwards. He grew restless, wanted only to get back to work and . . . forget. So he dusted off an old dream he'd had for this place, and set about making it a reality.'

Intrigued, she asked, 'What kind of dream?'

'Winterhaven had become a bit of a dinosaur, far too expensive to run simply as a home in this day and age. So he got the idea to turn the house into a sort of conference centre, and open up the gardens out back to the public.

'The bank likcd his plan and was happy to advance him a loan so that he could get to work on the project. But he'd underestimated the size of the job. The refurbishment of the house got so far, and then he ran out of money.

'He went back to the bank. They gave him more cash, took more of Winterhaven itself as collateral. Six months later he ran out of money again. And that's when he started to panic. He'd badly underestimated the cost of his plan, and couldn't bring himself to admit it, or ask for help, in case the bank decided to foreclose and take possession of the family home. So he concocted an elaborate charade to conceal the true extent of his panic. On the surface, everything appeared to be progressing well. But underneath, he was like a drowning man clutching at straws, and everything was slowly, inexorably slipping away from him. Eventually his various contractors ran out of patience and began to make justifiable demands for payment. He'd fobbed them off with promises for too long. But that only increased the pressure on him. How could he pay off his debts? He was virtually living on credit himself by then.'

He shook his head at the memory. 'In the end there was simply no way out. He *had* to face up to the situation. But before that could happen . . . '

It grew very quiet in the room, save for the crackling of the fire, and the odd popping of a log.

Annie cleared her throat. 'From the way you talk about him, you seem to have understood him very well, Donald,' she said.

'I *did* know him well,' he confessed.

With effort, he shrugged off the bleak mood into which he had fallen. 'Anyway, that's how the problem came about. Now all we have to do is see what can be done about solving it.'

She smiled encouragingly. 'The sooner I get started, the better, then.'

'Okay.' He snapped his fingers. 'Tell you what. I'll give you a guided tour of the place, and then make us some lunch.'

Warning bells sounded in Annie's head, for she knew it would be unwise to mix business with pleasure. 'Well . . .'

'Go on — I'm not a bad cook, and I'd appreciate the company.'

When she still hesitated to commit herself, he grew animated, obviously taken with the idea. 'Was my company really that bad on the train up from London yesterday?' he asked with a hangdog expression.

'It was wonderful,' she replied before she realised she had spoken.

It grew very quiet in the room then, and this time not even the crackling of the fire disturbed the stillness and silence. He looked at her, examining her features as if seeing her for the first time, and his fine-lined face grew very serious. 'Yes,' he said softly. 'It *was* wonderful.' He searched her face some more, and she felt herself colouring under his scrutiny. 'It's settled, then? You'll be my guest today?'

Surrender was sweet. 'I'd love to.'

After they finished their tea, he led her out into the hallway and began their tour with an inspection of the ground-floor rooms. The sun had come out again by then, so the house had a somewhat brighter appearance to it. Donald explained that his grandfather's original plan had been to hire out the large, well-lit rooms downstairs for company conferences, presentations and meetings, and hold the rooms on the first floor in readiness for any guests who might have to stay overnight. It had been his intention to retain private living quarters on the second floor.

And certainly Winterhaven seemed ideally suited to the purpose. Set amid the rolling, peaceful Scottish Highlands, off the beaten track and far away from the hurly-burly of city life, it was a place conducive to relaxation and learning.

The extensive gardens at the rear of the great house were also inspiring, when Annie finally got to see them a quarter of an hour later. They had obviously been landscaped by a genuine craftsman, and presented in such a way as to harness natural beauty with that cultivated by man. As a consequence, the gardens were an orderly riot of colour, with foxglove, kingcup, butterwort and wild iris growing beside white alyssum, fuschia and geraniums. Quaint stone paths flanked by Alpine plants led to rockeries, through pergolas and displays of shrubbery on to a miniature waterfall and picnic area bordered by a far-reaching stand of evergreens.

'Like it?' he asked after they came to a halt and stood side by side together to admire the vista.

'*Like* it?' she replied with a chuckle. 'Donald — it's marvellous.'

'Grandfather had to let our estate-keeper go when he couldn't afford to pay him any longer,' he confessed. 'But sooner or later I'm going to have to get another gardener in. To create such a work of art is one thing, but to maintain it is something else again!'

The ripple and sparkle of sunshine on water drew Annie's attention to a lake a few hundred yards away. It was a massive body of water, with gentle waves lapping at rugged banks, and more trees rising up out of the steep, grassy hills some distance to the west.

'How beautiful,' she whispered.

Donald said nothing, and his silence was grim. When she glanced up at him, she saw a gamut of emotions struggling for supremacy on his face. He was pale, tight-lipped; she saw his jaw-muscles working furiously, his eyes glazing as he focused almost unwillingly upon the distant loch.

'Donald?' she asked, frowning. 'Donald . . . are you all right?'

He gave no indication that he had heard the question, so she reached out to place one hand tenderly upon his arm, and at her touch he jumped, blinked, rejoined the land of the living with a jolt and gave a small, embarrassed smile.

'I'm sorry,' he said. 'It's just that . . . '

His voice trailed off and all at once she realised that this was the loch upon which his grandfather had drowned little more than a fortnight earlier. She remembered how he had described his grandfather back in the sitting room, as a drowning man clutching at straws. Now she realised he had meant that literally as well as metaphorically, and she shuddered slightly, wishing she had thought to be more diplomatic, and refrained from drawing his attention to the lake.

'Come on,' she urged. 'Show me the rest of the place.'

He forced himself to brighten up again. 'Okay.'

Andrew Logan's contractors had done a marvellous job on the ground floor of Winterhaven. The house was smart, orderly, dignified and majestic, filled with old world charm. By the time they had started work on the floors above, however, it had become obvious that Andrew was having financial difficulties, and so work had stopped. That explained why the first floor had appeared so derelict in comparison. Winterhaven had been in the middle of a complete refit; now it was suspended in limbo, awaiting the outcome of its uncertain fate.

At last they reached the third floor. The rooms up here, like those on the second floor, were rather shabby and obviously long-unused. But as Donald explained, this was where his grandfather had been hoping to establish his own personal quarters — a kitchen, sitting room, dining room, bedrooms and study.

'What a shame he wasn't able to see it through,' she murmured.

Donald nodded. 'His idea had some merit, didn't it?'

'Well, I can certainly see why his bank was so eager to approve it.'

They were standing in the last room along the corridor. It was comfortably large, and appeared larger because it was, at the moment, virtually empty of furniture. Now that the last of the clouds had fled northward the sun had reappeared, and it now cast pillars of dusty light in through the window to chase away the gloom. Standing there, Annie could see this room as a study, perhaps; a book-filled family room where the Logans might spend time together just reading or watching television or playing games or simply looking out over the estate. It struck her as tragic that, due to Andrew's mismanagement of his affairs, he had been unable to realise his dream, and had cast a blight upon Donald's happiness, too.

'Well,' Donald said at last, 'that's the lot. You've seen everything now. Any suggestions?'

She gave a small shrug. 'It's too early to say. I'll have to give it some thought and let you know.'

'Soon, I hope,' he said, and there was something in his voice, something low which gave her a pleasurable thrill, and told her he was referring more to their next meeting than to any decision she might make.

'Come on, then,' he said. 'Let's go and have lunch.'

'What are we having?'

He gave a careless shrug. 'Oh, I don't know. We'll see what's in the fridge, shall we?'

'*We?* I thought you said *you* were going to prepare lunch.'

He chuckled. 'All right — you choose; I'll cook. Fair enough? But *you* do the dishes afterwards.'

'We'll *both* do the dishes.'

'It's a deal.'

After lunch, which was more of a

light snack really, for Donald hadn't yet had the chance to get into Cairn Cawdor to do some shopping, they returned to the sitting room. The events of the day, coupled with the pleasant heat coming from the open fire, made Annie feel tired, but more than that, Donald's good company made her feel relaxed and welcome there. For a while, as they chatted about other things and discovered each other's likes and dislikes, time lost all meaning and relevance. They even forgot the circumstances which had brought them together. Eventually, though, the sun began its early slide into the west and the sky darkened in hue.

'I suppose I'd better be getting back to the hotel,' she said with some reluctance.

His disappointment was plain to see. 'Do you have to?'

'It'll be dark soon.'

'I'd drive you back myself, but I've only been back in the country a couple of days, and I haven't had the chance to rent or buy a car yet.'

'Oh, that's all right; if you'll point me towards your telephone, I can call the taxi-driver in the village to pick me up.'

He smiled suddenly and looked boyishly handsome in the fire's amber flicker. 'Tommy Roberts?' he said. 'Is he still in business? I thought he might have retired by now.'

'No. He brought me out here this morning.'

'They used to call him 'The Bogus Scotsman' in Cairn Cawdor. Do you know why?'

She nodded. 'Yes — because he was really born within the sound of Bow Bells!'

They laughed together, easily, comfortably, and then she went out into the hallway and dialled Tommy's number, and he said he would pick her up at the gates in about twenty minutes.

Donald fetched her coat, which had fortunately dried out nicely after its earlier soaking, and helped her into it. He had already donned a casual zip-up jacket of his own, in preparation for walking her down to the gates.

They left Winterhaven behind them, went down the steps and began to crunch softly back down the winding drive towards the road. The sky was a dusty blue-grey now, and shadows had thickened over the estate, thrown carelessly across grass and gravel alike by the towering trees. Annie could not help but glance nervously around them, remembering the figure she had seen, or *thought* she had seen, in the woods that morning.

Donald must have sensed her disquiet, because he offered her his arm and she was grateful for the comfort she took from just having him close.

'Will I see you again tomorrow?' he asked as they strolled arm-in-arm past the empty estate-keeper's cottage.

'I'll have to come back, of course,' she replied. 'In fact, I might well end up camping on your doorstep unless I can find lodgings elsewhere.'

He glanced at her profile. 'Eh?'

'The hotel closes for the winter tomorrow,' she explained. 'It doesn't reopen until March.'

He thought for a moment. 'Well, why *don't* you come and stay here?'

'Oh, no, I was only joking — '

'I know you were. But there's plenty of room. Surely it would make more sense for you to stay here than keep pestering poor old Tommy Roberts to drive you backwards and forwards every day?'

'Oh really, Donald, I couldn't.'

'Why not? Worried about the local gossip?'

'No, it's not that. It's just . . . '

'Look, just say the word, and I'll spend what's left of this evening getting one of the guest rooms ready for you.'

She thought about it. It would certainly solve the problem of finding alternative accommodation for the duration of her stay. And, as he said, it made more sense to be on site, as it were. But could she trust herself, spending so much time with him? He had a magnetic personality. When she was with him, time lost all meaning. She wondered how she would feel if she had to spend the better part of a week in his pleasurable company.

He was watching her, waiting for an answer, and she knew that sooner or later she would have to make a decision. Throwing caution to the wind, she finally said, 'All right, then. If you're certain it won't be an inconvenience.'

'Of course not!' he said, obviously delighted. 'I'd be glad of the company, for one thing.'

'Oh?' she asked, arching an eyebrow. 'And for another?'

He came to a halt and turned so that they were facing each other. She looked up into his shadowed face, her heart pounding wildly as he reached out, took a gentle hold on her arms and pulled her slowly towards him.

His face came down to meet hers, and she felt the heat coming off his flesh as their lips met, tentatively at first, tenderly, then took on more courage, pressed tighter, grew bolder, hungrier, more passionate.

She felt that this was a mistake, an error that went beyond mixing business with pleasure, for there was undoubtedly some deeper feeling within each of them, some commitment that one felt for the other. But his home was here, in the Highlands, while hers was a world away in London.

But in that moment there was no room for logic or common sense or caution or reason, there was only this dark, gravely drive with its rustling trees and soft, distant bird-cries, and this man, this young, attractive, generous, marvellous man who held her so safe in his arms, soothing her with his presence, soothing her, arousing her, *exciting* her, and filling her with love.

Their embrace seemed timeless and wonderful. Then, from someplace far, far away each of them slowly became aware of a car engine puttering in the distance but growing nearer, and as they broke apart, they saw the twin yellow beams of Tommy Roberts' old Hillman Minx rounding a bend in the narrow country road a few hundred yards away.

Annie looked up into Donald's eyes. They were hidden behind dark shadows. She wanted to say something to him, but was uncertain as to exactly what. Then he cleared his throat and said, 'I'm sorry if — '

She reached up and placed a finger on his lips and said, 'Shhh,' and he fell silent, but only for a moment. When he next spoke, it was to say, 'Will you come back tomorrow? To stay, I mean?'

She bobbed her head in the gloom. 'I . . . I'd like to,' she replied softly.

He relaxed visibly. 'Good . . . good. Well, then . . . '

The Hillman pulled up outside the gates some sixty yards away and Tommy Roberts gave a toot of his horn to attract her attention. Reluctantly Annie slipped from Donald's embrace and said, 'I'll see you in the morning, then . . . '

He nodded. 'I look forward to it.'

She peered up into his face, imprinting it upon her mind. 'Goodnight, Donald.'

He reached out impulsively to clasp one of her hands, which he then squeezed affectionately. 'Goodnight.'

She turned and hurried down the darkened drive towards the car.

4

Annie was not really aware of the drive back to Cairn Cawdor. Her mind was elsewhere.

Now that she was heading back to the village, the magical spell cast by the magnificent old house behind them began to desert her. She still felt light-headed, of course, for what had happened there in that shadowy drive-way had been both momentous and wonderful. But now that she was slowly returning to the real world, she began to wonder if she had made the right decision in accepting Donald's invitation to stay at Winterhaven.

She told herself that it would be madness to get too personally involved with what should, after all, have been merely a business associate. But wasn't it already a little too late for that? Like it or not — and she *did* like it — she was already involved; deeply so.

But where could her relationship with Donald lead? Nowhere. She felt that she should treat their affair much as one would treat a holiday romance; simply accept it for what it was and enjoy it for as long as it lasted, and at the end of it all, take away some fond and happy memories, and absolutely no regrets. But she knew even as she told herself as much, that she felt too strongly about Donald Logan for that. And, unless she was very much mistaken, he felt the same way about her.

Suddenly her business here was no longer straightforward, but had become infinitely more complex.

She was stirred from her introspection at that moment as the car slowed to a halt and Tommy said over his shoulder, 'I dunno. They've got all the street to park in, an' they still have pick the most awkward bloomin' spot they can find.'

Glancing up, Annie was surprised to

see that they had arrived back at the hotel. Peering ahead through the windscreen, she saw that he had been referring to a navy blue Porsche which had been parked carelessly — and illegally — outside the hotel entrance.

Annie paid the fare and climbed out of the car, pausing to ask him if he could pick her up again in the morning.

''Course,' he replied, good-naturedly. 'Back to Winterhaven again, is it?'

'Yes,' she said. 'To stay, this time. At least for the rest of the week.'

'Blimey,' he said. 'That was quick work, wasn't it?'

She forced a smile and agreed that it was. But as he edged around the Porsche and drove off, leaving her all alone there in the street, she thought about what he had said. It *had* happened quickly, all of it. Perhaps *too* quickly. She had only known Donald for a day and a half. The question that now plagued her was simply whether or not this feeling between she and

Donald would last, or end just as suddenly?

After a moment she shivered, for the early evening had turned chilly, and she hurried into the hotel.

Her host, the stout man with the sandy hair, blue eyes and ruddy complexion, was leaning against the desk, reading a paper, exactly as he had been the previous evening when she had first arrived. Again he looked up as the door closed behind her. Then he straightened up, set his paper aside and offered her a smile. 'Evening, Miss Tyler. Have a nice day, did ye?'

'Fine, thank you,' she said, accepting her key, and realising with a warm glow that the word *Fine* was an understatement.

'Good, good,' he said. But then his face sobered. 'I'm afraid I haven't had much luck finding ye someplace else to stay, miss,' he began apologetically.

'Oh, that's all right,' she said. 'I've made arrangements to stay up at Winterhaven.'

He was surprised. 'Have ye, miss? Master Donald come back home, then, has he?'

'Yes. Yesterday.'

He appeared to be genuinely relieved. 'So long as ye've found somewhere to stay.' Then he snapped his fingers. 'Oh, by the way, miss.'

'Yes?'

'There's a gentleman waiting to see ye in the bar.'

Annie frowned, for as far as she knew, only Mr Porter knew where to find her. 'Waiting to see *me?*' she repeated, just to make sure.

'Yes, miss. Asked for ye by name, he did. I told him ye'd gone out for the day and he said he'd wait. Been here most of the afternoon, he has.'

'He must want to see me quite badly, then,' she remarked. 'Did he give his name, by any chance?'

'Yes, miss. David O'Neal, it was. Ye can't miss him, if ye'd like to go through. He's a tallish fellow with short brown hair, and he's wearing a black suit.'

Annie's frown deepened. The name meant nothing to her. And yet the mysterious Mr David O'Neal obviously knew *her*. But curiosity quelled her irrational and probably groundless misgivings. 'I'd better not keep him waiting any longer, then,' she said.

She pushed through one of the doors in the wall to her left and entered a comfortable, softly-lit bar. Music played discreetly in the background, providing a relaxing accompaniment to the occasional clink of glasses and the pleasant buzz of conversation as a few local men and women socialised over drinks.

She spotted David O'Neal right away. The man would stand out in a crowd anywhere. He was, as the hotelier had said, a tall and striking figure, somewhere in his mid-twenties, clean-shaven, with neatly-combed brown hair, a rugged, lightly-tanned face and compelling hazel eyes. The cut of his suit was immaculate, its raven hue in stark contrast to the whiteness of his shirt and his pale grey tie. He was sitting on a stool at the bar, nursing a lager, working on some documents and occasionally tapping figures into a calculator, just killing time.

Annie wondered again who he was, and then decided there was only one way to find out. Taking a deep breath, she crossed the floor and came to a halt in front of him. 'Mr O'Neal?' she asked expectantly.

He turned around, focused on her, and appeared to recognise her. His smile widened out to reveal white, even, strong-looking teeth. 'Miss Tyler?' he said by way of reply. 'Annabel Tyler?'

She nodded. 'Yes. But I'm afraid you have me at a disadvantage.'

He stood up and offered her his hand. His palm was cool to the touch, but his grasp was firm. 'David O'Neal,' he said. 'Glengage Ltd. Please — will have a seat? Can I get you a drink?'

Annie moved to the stool beside his and said, 'Orange juice, please.'

He ordered and then retook his own

stool. 'I'm sorry to turn up unannounced like this,' he said. 'But I was told I might find you here.'

'Oh?' she said. 'By whom?'

'Your office in London,' he replied. He was softly-spoken, obviously well-educated, and there was only the slightest Scottish accent in his speech. 'I wonder — have you eaten at all today?'

'I had a snack earlier,' she said.

'Then you must be hungry again by now,' he decided. 'Good. I took the liberty of booking us a table next door. I hope you don't mind, but I thought that if we're going to discuss business, we might as well be civilised about it.'

She was somewhat taken aback by his invitation, but supposed there would be no harm in accepting. But what exactly was their business? She asked him.

He replied with one word. 'Winterhaven,' he said.

She frowned again. 'Winterhaven? I'm sorry, I don't understand . . . '

He glanced around them, and although they could not possibly be overheard, she knew he was trying to convey the impression that their business — whatever it might be — should be discussed in a more private atmosphere. 'Look, I've booked a table for seven-thirty.' He checked his watch. 'By my reckoning, that gives you a quarter of an hour to go up to your room, get your breath back and then meet me again next door.'

She studied him for a moment. She really did not know what to make of him. But she had to confess to her herself wryly that she *was* hungry, and she should be safe enough with him in a crowded restaurant.

'All right,' she said, setting down her glass. 'I'll meet you in just a little while.'

She hurried upstairs to her room, trying to make sense of this new twist. Why had the office given her whereabouts to this total stranger? Who was he, anyway? And what possible business could he have with her concerning Winterhaven?

Upstairs in her room, she took off her coat, quickly washed her face, reapplied make-up and brushed her short black hair. Then she went down to the restaurant and joined him at an intimate corner table.

The restaurant, like the bar, was softly-lit and patronised by several of the locals. Considering that it was a small and relatively out-of-the-way place, however, the menu appeared surprisingly ambitious. They ordered, and after the waitress fetched their aperitifs, Annie regarded David O'Neal speculatively. 'So,' she said. 'Don't think me ungracious, but what has any of this got to do with Winterhaven, Mr O'Neal?'

He grinned personably. 'It's David,' he said. 'And you don't believe in wasting time, do you? You just get right to the heart of the matter.'

'You've got me curious,' she replied.

'All right,' he said, taking a sip from his glass. He lowered his voice. 'I'm sure I don't need to tell you that news of Andrew Logan's death spread through the business community like wildfire. But accompanying that news was the revelation that he had run up some pretty hefty debts, and that someone from Porter, Sims and Johnson — *you, Annabel* — were coming up from London to see what could be done about sorting the whole mess out before Logan's grandson inherited the estate.'

'You seem to be remarkably well-informed,' she noted dryly.

He shrugged. 'It pays to be. Anyway, I've been looking into old man Logan's affairs myself. There's no way you're going to raise enough money to pay off all his debts, you know.'

'Oh?'

'How can you? There is very little of worth in the house itself.'

She glanced at him sharply. 'And how would you know that?' she demanded, more abruptly than she had intended.

'It's as you said,' he replied smoothly. 'It pays to be well-informed.'

She let that pass. 'Go on,' she said.

'Well, I take it you've been up to Winterhaven today. You must have looked around the place for yourself. Have you seen any marvellous treasures there which could be used to pay off any debts? Of course you haven't. So where does that leave you?'

'I'm confident that I can work something out.'

'I admire your confidence, then,' he said. 'But the banks are beginning to squeeze, Annabel. They want to get their money back and they're beginning to talk about foreclosing on Winterhaven. I've looked into this case thoroughly. There is no way you can raise enough money to clear the Logan debts before that happens . . . '

Their starters came then, and they fell silent while the waitress set two colourful prawn cocktails down on the table and then left them alone again.

Annie looked down at the food. Suddenly she had lost her appetite. She returned her own hazel eyes to his face and said, 'Exactly where is this all leading to, Mr O'Neal?'

'Oh, David, please. As I said — it's

nice to keep these things civilised if at all possible.'

'Exactly where is this all leading to?' she asked again, ignoring his invitation to call him by his Christian name. 'And who exactly do you represent?'

'All right,' he said, raising his palms in a gesture of surrender. 'Cards on the table. The company I represent, Glengage Ltd, is interested in buying Winterhaven. We will offer Donald Logan handsome terms for the property, more than enough to settle all his grandfather's debts and a little something besides. All you have to do is convince him that it is in his best interests to sell to us.'

She reached out and pushed the prawn cocktail away from her. She had definitely lost her appetite now. 'And why is Glengage so interested in Winterhaven?' she asked cautiously.

'Because the site has potential. And because Glengage is in the business of *realising* such potential.'

'Potential?' she repeated.

'Well,' he said expansively, 'we would have to develop the site considerably, of course, before it became suitable for our purpose.'

'Why?' she asked. 'What *is* your purpose?'

'That needn't concern you. That's all for the future, anyway.'

'I'm sorry, but I would need to know a bit more than that before I could possibly recommend such a course of action to Donald.'

He raised one eyebrow. 'Oh, it's 'Donald', is it?'

'What is that supposed to mean?'

'Nothing,' he said. He leaned forward across the table, and she fought the urge to lean backwards, away from him. 'You must understand that all business affairs have to be conducted confidentially, and on a need-to-know basis,' he said, attempting to make himself sound more reasonable. 'If word of our plans leaked out ... Well, I'm sure I don't need to draw you a diagram. We all have competitors. But let us be straight,

Annabel. You know as well as I do that there is precious little you can do to keep Winterhaven from the receivers. I — Glengage — is offering you a way out.'

'Winterhaven is Donald Logan's home,' she said. 'I couldn't recommend that he sell it just like that.'

'Not even for a small . . . ' he gestured vaguely with one hand as he searched for the right word, ' . . . shall we say 'consideration'?'

Her brows met in a mixture of puzzlement and disbelief. 'Are you attempting to bribe me, Mr O'Neal?'

He said, 'Shhh. People can get the wrong idea if you start using words like that, Annabel. And anyway, we don't like words like 'bribe'. They have nasty, unpleasant connotations.'

'Then what *are* you saying?'

'Simply that Glengage would obviously like to show its appreciation of your . . . co-operation, were you to persuade Donald Logan that it was in his best interests to sell the estate to us.'

She shook her head slowly. 'I don't believe that there is anything to be gained by prolonging this conversation, Mr O'Neal,' she said formally.

'David, please,' he reminded her. 'But think just a moment. What possible use can Winterhaven be to Logan's grandson? Good Lord, I should think the man would be glad to get rid of the place, given its history.'

'What history?' she asked suspiciously.

His brown eyes glittered. 'You mean you don't know about the curse?' he said.

Sensing that this was just another means of trying to talk her around, she lost patience with him again. 'Oh, this is ridiculous!'

'I assure you that there is nothing ridiculous about the curse of Winterhaven Loch,' he said gravely.

She searched his face, looking for that insolent gleam in his eye or the sardonic twist of his cynical mouth, but saw nothing. His sincerity appeared to be total, and was made all the more frightening because of it.

With effort she threw off the sudden chill his words had draped around her shoulders like a damp shawl. 'You can't frighten me into helping you do your dirty work, Mr O'Neal,' she said.

He only smiled. 'You know, I don't believe you're as confident as you make out,' he replied. 'In fact, you remind me of someone who jumps at shadows. Jumps, and runs like a rabbit.'

She wondered what he meant by that, and even as she wondered, so the answer came to her. She narrowed her eyes. 'It was *you*, wasn't it?' she said softly. 'Out there, poking around at Winterhaven this morning. It was you hiding in the woods!'

His expression became one of pure innocence. 'I'm sure I don't know what you're talking about. Winterhaven is private property. Do you think I look like the sort who'd trespass?'

'There is very little point in continuing with this conversation, Mr O'Neal,'

she said, irritated by his smug conde-
scension, his patronising, easy confidence.
'However, I do think you are right about
one thing.'

'Oh?'

'Yes. It *is* preferable to keep things on
a civilised basis whenever possible. That
is why I'm not going to submit to a
rather *un*civilised urge to take this
prawn cocktail and empty it onto your
head.' She stood abruptly. 'Goodnight,
Mr O'Neal. I trust we won't be meeting
again; Winterhaven is not for sale.'

'You'll change your mind about that,'
he predicted.

She turned on her heel, left the
restaurant and went straight back up to
her room, trembling with anger. The
nerve of the man, attempting to bribe
her into helping him get his hands on
Winterhaven! Who *was* he, anyway?
Who were Glengage? She decided that
she would find out in the morning.

She heard footsteps in the street
below and went over to the window.
She was just in time to see David

O'Neal leaving the hotel. He hurried across the pavement to the navy blue Porsche, almost tore the door open, climbed inside, fired the ignition and tore off with a squeal of rubber and smoke.

Perhaps he wasn't so sure she would change her mind after all.

* * *

She found sleep difficult that night. But that was hardly surprising. So much had happened in so short a space of time.

After a couple of hours she gave up even trying, and sat up, switched on the bedside lamp and padded into the bathroom to pour herself a glass of water. As she came back out again, she saw that a low mist had settled across Cairn Cawdor. It rose and fell and swirled slowly like the diaphanous folds of a shroud.

The analogy made her shudder, and she found herself remembering what

David O'Neal had said earlier, about the curse of Winterhaven Loch. She tried to shrug it off, dismiss it as nonsense. But Andrew Logan had drowned in that loch. And Donald had found even the very sight of it distressing.

She concluded that O'Neal had probably made the story up to try and convince her that Donald would be better off selling the estate. After all, this was the twenty-first century, an age of reason and science, not superstition. There were no such things as curses anymore, even assuming that there ever had been, in some dark, distant past.

But O'Neal was right in one respect. The Logan debts *were* large, frighteningly so, and so far she was no nearer to finding a possible way to solve them. She could not bring herself to even consider the prospect that Donald might yet lose his ancestral home, but unless some miracle occurred, she knew that this remained a very real probability.

Her thoughts turned again to Donald, and she found comfort in picturing him in her mind; his generous height and build, the bronzed, fit tan of his skin, the azure depths of his blue eyes, the way his short dark-blonde hair twisted and curled and showed golden when the autumn sun caught it at just the right angle. She knew without any shadow of doubt that she was in love with him. But again she wondered if it was a love that could possibly last?

Eventually her eyelids began to grow heavy and she felt that sleep was finally coming to claim her. She didn't remember dozing off, but the next time she opened her eyes, sunlight was streaming in through the window and the bedside alarm clock said that it was a quarter to eight.

Annie climbed out of bed, showered and went downstairs to breakfast. She had made arrangements for Tommy Roberts to pick her up at ten o'clock, so she had plenty of time to pack her things and do what she could to find out exactly who or what Glengage Ltd really was.

By the time she had finished repacking, it was a little after nine o'clock. Using the phone in her room, she dialled her office in London, knowing from experience that the staff usually made it a point to get into work long before their start-time of nine-thirty.

She was right. The phone was answered at the other end on the second ring, and Kim Hill's voice came clearly into her ear.

'Good morning, Porter, Sims and Johnson. Can I help you?'

'Hello, Kim, it's Annie.'

'Annie! How *are* you? What are things like in Bonnie Scotland?'

'Well, I haven't seen any men wearing kilts yet, if that's what you mean.'

Kim laughed. 'Oh well, it's still early days. I'll keep my fingers crossed for you.'

'Is Mr Porter in yet, by any chance?'

'He is. Hang on, I'll put you through.'

There was a click, and then Clive Porter's voice came on the line. 'Hello, Annie?'

'Good morning, Mr Porter.'

'How are things progressing?'

Annie echoed what Kim had said a few moments earlier. 'Well, it's early days yet. But I've met Donald Logan. He took me on a guided tour of Winterhaven yesterday, but to be honest, I'm at a loss as to how we're going to resolve this business, really. There doesn't seem to be much room for manoeuvre.'

'I was afraid of that,' Clive Porter said quietly.

'But as I say, it's early days yet. What I'm really phoning about is this fellow David O'Neal.'

'And who's he?' Mr Porter asked.

Annie was a bit surprised by the question. 'He represents a company called Glengage Ltd. They're very interested in trying to buy Winterhaven, apparently. He said he spoke to someone there yesterday, and they told him where to find me.'

'We've had no enquiries about Winterhaven from anyone at this end,' Mr Porter said, his voice mystified. 'What did you say his name was?'

Annie told him again, but it struck no chord. 'You've never heard of these people Glengage Ltd, then?' she asked.

'No. But I'll make a few enquiries at this end and see what I can turn up. Meanwhile, if this fellow O'Neal approaches you again, don't even give him the time of day. Call for the police and have him dragged away.'

'Oh, I don't think he's dangerous,' she replied. *Or did she?* After that business yesterday morning, when he had hidden in the woods, she wasn't so sure. 'But I was just curious as to why he was so keen to buy the estate.' She sighed. 'Anyway, I'd better be going. But I'll keep you posted with developments.'

'All right, Annie. Take care.'

She rang off and then, on impulse, decided to ring the operator and ask if there was any number listed for Glengage Ltd. She was in luck; there was.

She jotted it down on her notepad, rang off and then dialled the number. A switchboard girl with a strong Highland accent answered after a while and asked her which extension she wanted.

'Actually, I don't want *any* extension,' Annie replied. 'I just wanted to know what line of business Glengage is in.'

It was obviously an unusual query, but the girl at the other end of the phone seemed happy enough to divulge that Glengage was involved with sports and leisure facilities.

But did that help to solve the puzzle, or merely muddy the waters still further? Annie wasn't sure, but just to make sure she had the right company, she asked if there was a Mr David O'Neal on the staff. The switchboard girl said that there was. 'Do you want me to put you through to him?' she asked.

'Oh, no, that's all right,' Annie replied hurriedly. 'But thank you very much, anyway.' And she rang off.

Sports and leisure facilities? And this company was interested in buying Winterhaven? She wasn't really sure what to make of it.

But there was no time to ponder it just now. A quick glance at her wristwatch told her that time was marching on, and that Tommy Roberts would be here at any moment. She gathered together her luggage and was halfway to the door when the strap on her flight bag broke again and the bag itself dropped to the carpet.

Muttering irritably, Annie bent to scoop the fallen bag up. Obviously the temporary repair she had effected on the damaged buckle had been exactly that — temporary. She would have to find some way of making the repair more permanent. She paused for just a moment, remembering the first time it had happened, and how, as she had bent to retrieve it, Donald's shadow had fallen across her. Just thinking about that first meeting gave her a warm feeling inside; the prospect of seeing him again very, very soon made her feel positively radiant.

She went downstairs and settled her bill. The hotelier was still very apologetic about not being able to board her longer, but she told him not to worry about it.

'Well, then, miss, all the best to you,' he said, reaching across the desk to shake her hand. 'I hope you enjoy the rest of your stay up at Winterhaven.'

5

Tommy Roberts' Hillman rolled up not very long afterwards, and the big, good-natured Cockney got out of the car to help her with her luggage. 'In you get, princess,' he said as he stowed her things in the boot.

The drive out to Winterhaven didn't take very long, and this time Tommy turned in through the gates and drove slowly up the gravel drive, tyres crunching and spitting stones beneath them. In the back seat, Annie felt her sense of anticipation rising. Now that she was back on the estate, the magical influence of Winterhaven began to exert itself over her once more.

'The Bogus Scotsman' drew the car to a halt before the great, grey-stone and ivy-clad house and climbed out to get her luggage. By the time he had placed her suitcase and flight bag on the stone steps beside the front door, Annie had also alighted. She paid the fare and thanked him for all his help.

'My pleasure, love,' he said warmly. Glancing up at the house, he remarked, 'Big old place, innit?' The structure was reflected and distorted in the thick lenses of his glasses.

'You should see it from the inside,' she agreed.

He studied its regal lines for a moment longer, then said, 'Well, I suppose I'd better be getting along. Got any idea when you'll be going back home yet?'

'Not really. It's . . . it's a bit difficult to say.'

'Well, you've got me number,' he said. 'Just let me know when you want me to come out and run you back to the station.'

'I will, Tommy. Thanks for all your help.'

As he drove away she climbed the steps and worked the bell-pull. A few moments later the door swung open and Donald stood there, tall, lithe, athletic in an open-necked blue shirt beneath which he wore a white tee-shirt, and smart black trousers.

His face lit up when he saw her, but his greeting was somewhat less than enthusiastic. 'Ah, Annie,' he said in a curiously flat tone, reaching down to collect together her baggage. 'In you come.'

She crossed the portal with a disconcerted frown playing over her brow. She had been sure of receiving a warmer welcome than this, especially given the nature of their parting last night. This rather cool reception had come as a nasty surprise, and hurt her more deeply than she could say.

She wondered what was wrong, if he were all right, if perhaps she had unwittingly done something amiss. 'I'm not too early, am I, Donald?' she asked carefully.

'Early? Oh, no. No. Not at all.' He stood there in the vast hallway, holding her luggage, looking awkward and wretched. 'I . . . ' He hesitated a moment, then said, 'Here, let me show you to your room.'

They ascended the wide stairway, footsteps echoing up through the great house. He seemed to be very animated, as if he were trying too hard to pretend that everything was all right. She felt her heart go out to him, knowing that he must be under a terrible strain, what with the prospect of losing his family home constantly hanging over him, and she wished that she could do something to ease his burden.

'I think you'll like the room I've chosen,' he said over one shoulder. 'It overlooks the gardens.'

'Thank you,' she said in a small, uncertain voice.

They reached the first floor corridor and he stopped at the first door he came to and, because his hands were full, he worked the handle awkwardly with one elbow. The door swung open and he stood aside to allow her entrance. She brushed past him, wanting to enjoy the brief closeness but sensing that he had somehow erected an invisible barrier between them.

He had worked wonders with the room, though, for it was as bright and spotless as the rooms on the ground floor, and in far better repair than the other rooms on this floor or the one above.

It was undoubtedly a lady's room. The wallpaper was a cheerful pink, the furniture delicate, ornate, much of it antique but in excellent condition. Daylight filtered in through chalk-white lace curtains that were flanked by heavier, richer, deeper pink drapes. An old fourposter bed dominated the room. It looked huge. He had chosen the room for its beauty, she knew, and he must have worked half the night to have made it so habitable for her. She wanted to turn and thank him and enjoy the same warmth and intimacy they had shared the previous evening, but felt, for some strange and indefinable reason, that she daren't.

Instead she just turned to face him and said, 'It's lovely, Donald.'

She watched him take her bags across to the dressing table facing the bed and set them down. She could not bear for them to behave so formally together, and wanted to know what had gone wrong between them, what she or he or *they* could do to put it right. 'Donald,' she said, speaking before she could think about it too much and then decide not to say anything at all. 'What is it? What's wrong?'

He tried to appear puzzled. 'Wrong? Nothing's wrong.'

But she didn't believe him any more than he believed himself. 'Has something happened?' she asked, coming closer. 'Something I should know about?'

He shrugged. 'There was a letter this morning,' he said, reaching into his back pocket to draw it out and pass it over to her. 'It's from the bank. They've had enough. They want to know what I intend to do to clear my grandfather's debts, and they're making it plain that if they don't like what I have to say to them, they plan to instigate proceedings to take possession of the house.'

She scanned the letter quickly. The sheet of paper trembled in her unsteady grasp. All at once she thought she understood the reason for his subdued mood. The pressure was mounting, as David O'Neal had said it would. And not only did she have to find some way of helping Donald to keep possession of Winterhaven — she was going to find herself working against the clock to do it.

'When do they want to see you?' she asked.

'On Friday.'

'And do you have any idea what you're going to tell them?'

'No. All I can do is ask for more time. That, and pray that something turns up in the meantime.'

'Oh, Donald . . . ' She felt such

compassion for this handsome young man that she went towards him, wanting to comfort him and assure him that everything would be all right, but to her surprise, he took a step away from her. She froze where she was, glanced at him, puzzled and hurt, and although she saw from his expression that he took no pleasure from keeping his distance, it was scant consolation.

'There *is* something else,' he said hesitantly.

She studied him silently, waiting for him to carry on, dreading what she thought he was about to say and not trusting herself to speak.

'It . . . it's about you and me,' he said at last, swallowing in his anxiety. 'I'm sorry, Annie. What I did . . . what *we* did . . . last night was . . . a mistake. I never should have been so presumptuous or forward, taken advantage . . . '

She shook her head, because this was the last thing she wanted to hear. 'No, Donald. You didn't take advantage of me. That didn't even come into it. I *wanted* you to kiss me. I wanted to kiss *you*. I thought . . . ' She wasn't exactly sure how to say what she wanted to say next. She felt foolish, telling him that she was in love with him, having only known him such a brief time, and though she was still certain that he felt the same way about her, there was always the chance that she had read the signs wrong, that nothing had been further from his mind that thoughts of love.

'I behaved unforgivably,' he said stiffly. 'But I just couldn't help myself.' He made a gesture of frustration. 'Look, just . . . forget it. *Please*. The way things stand at the moment, I think anything other than a purely business-like relationship would be . . . unwise. I'm sorry. But I think we should put what happened between us last night out of our minds.'

His words were like a knife ripping into her heart and twisting without mercy. Suddenly, as she withdrew into herself, the room took on an unreal aspect, as if this were really a dream — a *nightmare* — and that if she were to try crossing the floor, or reaching out to touch the walls, she would discover that they were really made of rubber.

All at once, an unpleasant thought came into her head. 'Is it that . . . I mean . . . are you already married? Or engaged?'

'No.'

'Then what is it?' she persisted. And then, for no real reason other than that it occurred to her at precisely that moment, she said, 'Is it because of the curse?'

His glance was sharp and furtive. 'What? What was that? What do you know about the curse?'

She began to come back down to earth again. 'Nothing,' she said defeatedly. 'Nothing important, anyway.' She ran her eyes over his face, seeing him in a new light. 'Nothing's important, is it, Donald? Except saving Winterhaven?'

He shook his head in frustration. '*You're* important. To me. But I've hurt you enough already,' he said miserably. 'I don't want to hurt you any more. Please believe that, Annie.'

Unable to speak now as emotion welled up and threatened to choke her, she could only nod and turn away from him. A moment later she heard him crossing the floor, leaving the room and closing the door softly behind him.

At last she allowed the shortness of breath she had been holding back to go free, and she stumbled blindly towards the bed, where she sat down and buried her face in her hands.

She felt confused, disappointed and humiliated. How could she have known such happiness with him yesterday, and such misery today? Again she tried to tell herself that he was under pressure. But what if the *real* truth was very much different; that she *had* read the signs wrong, that he didn't love her, that perhaps he had seen their relationship more as a casual holiday romance, and decided to draw it to an end when he realised that she had read more into it than he had intended?

Emotion drained her and left her exhausted. Tiredly she dried her tears and sat there in the bright, cheerful pink room feeling hollow. Yesterday she had been wondering if their love could last. Now she had her answer.

There was one problem, though. For while he evidently did not love *her*, she could not stop loving *him*.

She stood up and left the room to visit the bathroom, where she washed her face in cold water and bathed her eyes, which her salty tears had made sore. She wasn't sure exactly where their confrontation left her now. It was certainly going to make their relationship here over the next week or so more difficult.

She returned to her bedroom, saw that he had evidently tried to pay her a visit during her absence and left a cup of tea steaming away on the bedside cabinet.

Her thoughts turned to the house. Caught up in the heady, wonderful euphoria of falling in love, Winterhaven had taken second place in her priorities. Now she decided to give it *top* priority, find a way of helping Donald settle his grandfather's debts, and then return to London as soon as possible and put this entire affair behind her.

She knew that she should try to occupy herself with the task that had brought her up to Scotland in the first place, but her heart just wasn't in it, and she feared that any error she might make in her present fragile, preoccupied state might only make things worse. Since it was a fine morning, she decided to go out for a walk. Hopefully, the air might clear her head.

She changed from her skirt and blouse into more suitable attire; a shirt, jeans and trainers, and slipped into a thick, waist-length suede jacket. Within a few minutes she had left her room and descended the stairs.

She met Donald just coming out of the sitting room. He saw that she was wearing a jacket and said, 'You're not leaving . . . ?'

'No,' she said in a shaky voice. 'Although I will, if you'd prefer it.'

'I wouldn't,' he said at once.

'I just thought I'd go for a little walk before I start work.'

He nodded. 'Ah, yes. I see.'

She left the old house behind her.

She was headed for nowhere in particular. She just wanted to walk, take in the clear, fresh air, try to outdistance her problems, perhaps get them all into perspective and then return to Winterhaven with some small measure of peace of mind. So she did exactly that; she walked, and lost all sense of time and distance.

Still her thoughts were in turmoil, though. There were so many of them that her mind felt crammed full. She knew there was nowhere she could go to where they would not follow and plague her. Suddenly she wanted only to be back home, among friends, away from this place.

She looked up from her reverie, deciding that she had walked far enough. According to her wristwatch, in fact, she had been out far longer than she had intended. She turned around, intending to head back to Winterhaven. But it was only then that she realised she had not really been paying much attention to where she had been going, and now, although she hated to admit it, it appeared that she had gotten herself lost.

'Oh, no,' she sighed softly.

She had left the lane some distance back. She remembered that much, at least. Ahead of her had been a swell of land covered with thick, rich grass and stippled with cuckoo flowers and forget-me-nots. Now she was on the far side of that swell, in an emerald green glen that stretched as far as she could see in both directions, misty in the distance, its only occupants some fearsome-looking but mild-mannered Highland cattle. Ahead rose another hill, studded with the odd tree and scattered grey boulders. And to make matters worse, the fine morning had clouded up and some of those clouds now gathering overhead were swollen and purple, presaging another of the periodic downpours she had come to expect in the past couple of days.

Stuffing her hands deep into the pockets of her jacket, for the wind had picked up raw and biting, she turned around and tried as best she could to retrace her steps. It was hard work to reach the top of the hill. She marvelled at the fact that she had been so deep in thought before, she had no memory of negotiating it in the first place.

But when she reached the summit, the country lane she had been hoping to find on the other side was nowhere in sight. Instead, a stream chuckled and bubbled over smooth oval stones along the valley-floor below, fringed by golden wildflowers and trees.

She saw a few sheep grazing several hundred yards away to her left. That was something, she thought. There might be someone nearby from whom she could get directions.

She came down the far side of the hill, listening to the sounds of the birds in the trees, watching as frogs hopped and leapt through the bracken and cormorants, lapwing, curlews and oystercatchers foraged in among the damp grass, looking for food.

White spray flew through the air as the stream chuckled on past. It was a beautiful, serene spot. On a nicer day, and under better circumstances, it would have made an ideal picnic spot, a place so far removed from the rest of the world that one really *could* leave all of his or her cares behind them.

But Annie had other considerations just then, because the day seemed to be growing duller and darker, the shapes of the sheep in the distance growing fainter, more blurred . . .

She realised with a nasty jar that a mist was rolling in from the far end of the glen, and gradually thickening up. The revelation sent a chill down her spine, for she dearly did not want to be caught out here in this exposed, desolate place cocooned in a blanket of fog.

She picked up her pace and continued tramping across the shaggy, craggy bank towards the sheep, still a couple of hundred yards away. Mist swirled and churned around her legs as she waded on through it, her personal problems temporarily supplanted by this more immediate complication.

Somewhere in the distance she heard a bird crying raucously. The sound intensified her feeling of isolation. She knew that she must reach either the lane or a farm soon, that she couldn't have wandered *too* far off her original course, but there was something about this glen now, with its utter peace and solitude and its rainclouds gathering above and its ever-thickening mist, that made her feel somehow vulnerable.

At last the mist grew so thick that she had to slow her pace and draw out a handkerchief to hold over her nose and mouth. She knew she had been a fool to lose herself like this, but knowing that now hardly helped to improve her situation.

Then the grass beneath her feet began to thin out and she realised with an overwhelming sense of relief and gratitude that she had somehow reached a footpath, and that the footpath must lead *somewhere*. Provided she was careful and didn't stray from it again, she should eventually reach civilisation.

The mist fairly congealed around her, muffling her footsteps and all the other country-sounds had started growing used to. She began to feel panicky, claustrophobic, but fought against the urge to hurry. If she should stumble from the footpath, she would never find it again in these conditions.

Then she heard a sound somewhere up ahead, and came to a stop. There — again! It sounded like the heavy tread of a large, bulky man, and he appeared to be coming towards her.

The events of the day had already

made her over-sensitive, and she realised just how silly she had been to come out to this remote spot all alone. But now she heard those footsteps coming closer and she knew that they had not been a figment of her imagination.

She took the handkerchief from her mouth and called out an experimental, 'Hello?'

The crunching, ponderous footfalls came to a halt somewhere out in front of her.

'Hello?' she heard the tremor in her voice and knew that she was very scared now. 'Is anyone there?'

The footsteps started up again, crunch . . . crunch . . . crunch . . . crunch . . . slowly coming forward, heavy, deliberate, remorseless.

'Hello?' The word came out sharp and high.

A silhouette appeared through the mist. She narrowed her eyes to sharpen upon it. A big man with wide, sloping shoulders, coming nearer, nearer . . .

'Who's that?' he asked suddenly. His voice sounded mild and curious and well-intentioned.

Before she could answer, he loomed large and misty-dark in front of her, a giant of a man, with a broad, barrel chest and enormously thick and very long arms. She drew in a sharp, startled breath behind the handkerchief, for he had closed the last remaining few feet between them in silence.

He had long, shaggy blond hair and a thick beard that was slightly darker. His dark eyes were opened wide now in surprise, for clearly he had not expected to find a young girl out here all alone. He was in his thirties, she thought, quite pleasant in a weathered, rustic fashion.

'Why, who are *you?*' he asked in a surprisingly gentle voice. 'What are ye doin' way out here in the mist, girl?'

'I'm lost,' she said simply.

He accepted this with a business-like nod. 'Well, ye'd best come back home wi' me till this mist lifts.'

'Oh, I don't want to impose. If you could just point me towards the main road I'll be all — '

'Awa' wi' ye, now. I'd say ye could do with a nice hot cup o' tea an' a wee sit by the fire to warm yeself through afore ye think about goin' anyplace else.' He smiled. 'Come along, now. Ma mother'll be pleased tae fuss over ye.'

He turned back the way he had come and guided her further long the footpath, moving confidently through the fog. Obviously he knew the area well and did not even think to question or check the direction in which he trudged.

'So ye got y'sen lost, did ye?' he said, glancing down at her. 'Well, ye're not all that far from the road. Come far?'

'From Winterhaven.'

His voice showed interest. 'Oh aye? Ye've come a fair piece, then. Winterhaven's aboot three or four miles back down the way there, headin' towards Cairn Cawdor. Tell you what; once this mist lifts, I'll given ye a lift back on the tractor.'

'That's all right. You've been kind enough already. But I won't say no to that offer of a cup of tea.'

The footpath grew rougher and stonier and soon she could make out the dim shapes of farm buildings. The clucking of hens and the bleating of sheep soon confirmed that he was a crofter, and that they had reached his property. They came down off the path and entered a yard. A single-storey house loomed up before them and he went on ahead to open the front door for her.

The room into which she stepped was a combination kitchen, dining room and sitting room. The air was warm and smelled of homebaked cakes and pastries. A grey-headed old woman wearing old-fashioned wire-framed spectacles was busying herself at the antiquated range. She was short, portly, in her late seventies, with a ruddy, kind-natured face, a rather overlarge nose and a very, very pleasant smile. She eyed Annie with some surprise, wiping floury hands on the smock she wore over her old print dress, until the large man, her son, closed the door behind him and said, 'Look what I fetched home, mother. I found the young lady wandering up the glen a-ways.'

The old woman frowned. 'Wanderin' in this weather, hen?'

'I went for a walk and got lost,' Annie explained sheepishly. 'Before I could find my way back to the road, I got caught in the fog.'

'Well, come in an' set yourself down there by the fire. I have some tea brewin'. Will ye stop for a cup, Kenneth?'

The big man shook his head. 'Nae. I'd best find the last o' the strays before the rain comes.'

'Well, thank you for all your help,' Annie said.

He blushed. 'Och, that's all right. The young lady's come all the way from

Winterhaven, ma.'

The old woman showed interest at this statement. 'Aye? I'd have said ye'd come a bit further than that, judgin' by your accent.'

Annie smiled. 'I have. London. But I'm staying up at Winterhaven for a few days, on business.'

'Aye,' the old woman said again. 'I knew that old Andrew's death would cause ructions, if all the gossip's to be believed.'

As Kenneth let himself out again, Annie unbuttoned her jacket and skirted the pine table and chairs in the centre of the room to take one of the lumpy old chairs beside the open fire. 'Do ye have a name, hen?' the old woman asked.

'Annie,' she replied.

'Well, Annie, my name is Rachel McFarlane, and that big lump there was my son, Kenneth. Here, my love, drink your tea while it's hot.'

Annie accepted the cup with a nod of thanks. 'This really is very kind of you . . . ' she began.

'Away with ye! It's not fit oot there for man nor beast when the mist comes down like this.'

Annie turned her attention to the fire for a moment, enjoying the strong taste of the tea and the sensation of warmth and life slowly ebbing back into her chilled limbs.

The old woman poured herself a cup of tea and came over to join her. She eased herself slowly into a chair, and allowed herself a sigh of contentment once she was settled. Annie felt the old woman's eyes studying her shrewdly for a while. Then Rachel MacFarlane said, 'You're troubled, aren't ye, hen.' It was a statement, not a question.

Annie was startled by the pronouncement and immediately made to deny it. 'Just cold,' she replied, forcing a smile. 'And I must admit, I was starting to get a little frightened out there on the footpath before your son came to my rescue.'

'I don't mean *that*,' Rachel said. 'I

mean *in y'sen*. Troubled. Worried. I can
tell. I have the gift.'

'Gift?'

The old woman nodded and winked.
'The gift of second sight.' she explained.
She reached forward and put one cal-
loused, large-veined hand upon Annie's
arm. 'Oh, I don't mean tae be personal.
Tell me tae mind ma own business, if ye
like. But it's as I said, I can tell these
things.' She studied Annie for a moment
longer and then smiled. 'It's a man,
isn't it?'

'I'd rather not say,' Annie replied.

'As ye will,' Rachel said without
taking offence. 'But don't ye fret. It'll
all work out.'

Without warning, the old woman
shrugged and changed the subject. 'So
— ye've come up from London, have
ye? How long have ye been in the
Highlands?'

'Only a few days.'

'And what do you think of the place?'

'The countryside is wonderful,' Annie
said honestly. 'You know, living and

working in London, you forget that such places still exist. And as for the people . . . ' She indicated her cup. 'I've found them to be very generous and warm-hearted.'

'Aye, well, that's very kind of ye tae say so.'

Something occurred to Annie then, and now she tried to find a way of broaching the subject. Rachel MacFarlane was old, had lived in these parts probably all of her life, and given her reference to 'the gift of second sight', it was just possible that she might know of . . . other things.

'I've heard some talk since I've been here,' she said, trying to word her request casually. 'Something about a curse on Winterhaven?'

'Oh aye,' said the old woman, with an immediate nod.

'I wonder . . . do you know anything about it?'

Rachel eyed her strangely. 'It could be that ye're better off not knowin' about such things, hen.'

'I was just curious.'

'Well, there *is* a curse, right enough. But . . . '

'Please, Rachel. I'd like to find out more about it, if I can.'

'Is it that important to ye?'

'I don't know . . . but it could be.'

The old woman peered into the fire, with its flickering, ever-changing patterns, and slowly drank from her cup. 'Well, let me say at the outset that it's not a pretty story. And let me make it plain that I dinna believe in spells and curses maself. These events *did* happen, o'course. But it's only human nature to read more intae 'em than is actually there. Do ye understand what I'm sayin', hen?'

'You're saying that I shouldn't take any of it very seriously,' Annie replied.

'Ye shouldna take it too seriously,' Rachel confirmed. 'An' neither should ye necessarily take it *to heart*.'

She gathered her thoughts. 'This so-called curse started some two or three centuries ago, with the first of the

144

Logans to own the estate, a Godless, jealous man by the name of William Logan. Old William, he never could bring himself to trust his wife, who was a beautiful woman and whom, in the days before she got married, had had many admirers.

'In *his* day, William had been something of a rake and a libertine, but his Hester was a Godly woman, and was faithful to him. But as I say, William could never bring himself to trust her, or anyone else if it comes tae that, completely. Because he himself was so corrupt in his ways, he believed that everyone was just as bad as he.

'Anyway, a few months into their marriage, Hester fell pregnant, as was to be expected, and at first, old William was overjoyed, for what man dinna want an heir to carry on his family's name? But over the months, something dark came intae his soul. Doubt. He began to suspect that he was not the father of the unborn child, and would believe none of Hester's protestations to the contrary.

'As the weeks went past, so he grew more and more convinced that Hester's baby was not his. Finally, on the night she gave birth to the wee bairn, he drank himself into a rage and took the baby out to the loch and drowned it.'

Annie went cold. 'My God,' she muttered.

'Aye, and that was where the curse began, with that foul deed. William committed suicide shortly afterwards, unable to live with the guilt of his actions, and his brother Robbie came tae live at Winterhaven. By all accounts he was a kinder, more God-fearing man, was Robbie Logan, and he looked after Hester as best he could, but she was never the same woman after William took her baby away from her, and she ended her days deranged.

'Well, you know how people are. From that time on, any calamity or misfortune, no matter how small, was ascribed tae the curse. And that's how the legend built up. They say that love cannot flourish at Winterhaven, though I don't hold with that one little bit, for love, *true* love, can conquer all. But certainly over the years the Logans have had more than their share of trouble.

'You take poor Master Donald, for instance. Lost both his parents in a plane crash when he was just eight years of age, he did, and his grandmother — Andrew Logan's wife — not so very long after that. Andrew did the best he could for the boy, o'course, but he never truly got over losing his wife. And, do you know, I was so pleased when I heard that he'd picked up with another woman — she came up from London as well, come tae think of it — but even there bad luck dogged him, and she died, too. And then, o'course, there was Andrew himself, dying the way he did . . . '

It went quiet after the old woman's gentle, lilting voice dried up, and Annie sat for a time thinking over her words. *They say that love cannot flourish at*

Winterhaven . . . Was that what Donald truly believed? Was that why he had told her that they must put what had happened out of their minds? If that was the case, then she must return to him, tell him that he was wrong, repeat to him what Rachel had just said to her, that love, *true* love, could conquer all.

'I told ye it wasna a pretty story, Annie,' the old woman said. 'Do ye feel any the better now for havin' heard it?'

Annie looked at her, saw her own face reflected in the woman's glasses. 'Yes,' she said slowly. 'Yes, Rachel. Strangely enough, I think I do.'

And suddenly she found herself willing the mist to lift so that she could set off back to Winterhaven, and Donald; so that she could tell him exactly that one, unassailable truth — that true love *could* conquer all.

6

A brief shower half an hour later helped to disperse some of the lingering fog, and not so very long after that the mist began to thin out. Annie rose from her cosy spot by the fire and offered her thanks to Rachel MacFarlane for all her hospitality, then said that she must be going.

'Are ye sure, hen?' the old woman asked. 'It's quite a walk back to Winterhaven, ye know. Kenny would be happy to drive ye back on the tractor as soon as he gets in.'

'No, really. I could stop here and chat with you all afternoon, but you've already been kind enough as it is.'

The old woman shrugged. 'Och, well . . . '

'If I could just trouble you for some directions . . . '

Rachel showed her to the door and

they stepped out into the yard. The daylight was still weak and hazy, but better than it had been, and a few moments later, following the old woman's directions, Annie set off back towards Winterhaven.

Now that she thought she understood why Donald had behaved as he had, she felt somewhat easier in her mind. He had probably grown up with the legend of the curse, and never thought to question its veracity or validity. The death of his parents and the death of his grandmother shortly afterwards had probably only served to reinforce it in his impressionable young mind. Now that she could appreciate that, she could begin the process of helping him to see it for himself, prove to him that love *could* thrive in this remote Scottish locale, regardless of superstition.

She followed a rutted path out of the yard, turning back once to throw Rachel MacFarlane a cheery wave, and then found her way out onto the peaceful lane.

As she walked, the afternoon sun gradually strengthened and chased away the last of the mist. Clouds still gathered darkly in the far distance, however, stacking together like high, unclimbable mountains, but at least further rain held off as she trudged back the way she had come.

At last parts of the countryside began to look familiar to her, and she realised with some relief that she was nearing the end of her journey. Spotting a gap in the hedge, and believing that it might offer a short-cut back to the big house, she squeezed through and continued her hike down across a grassy slope stippled with buttercups and the odd, darker green patch of clover.

Just on the other side of a hedgerow some hundred and fifty yards away, she saw the house with its turreted towers and ivy-draped walls, and smiled. She was just about to pass what appeared to be some disused out-buildings when she heard a sound from inside one of them.

She frowned and slowed to a stop, wondering for just a moment if she had heard the sounds of scurrying rats. But then she heard another noise, something, some large piece of junk or clutter, being pushed aside, and knew that it wasn't rodents.

The sheds looked to be in a poor state of repair, although the roofs appeared sound enough. Was it possible then, that some passing vagrant had spotted them and decided to occupy one? If so, he might live here undisturbed for weeks or even months, for obviously the place was seldom visited.

On impulse she decided to go closer and find out. When she was standing right in front of the dilapidated shed from which she had heard the sounds, she said, 'Who's in there?' She tried to force some authority into her tone, knowing that she had been foolish to encourage a possible confrontation with a tramp, and that she should make some attempt to control the situation right from the outset.

It was very quiet inside the shed.

'Who is it?' she demanded sharply.

She waited a moment, her tiny fists clenching and unclenching as tension buzzed through her. She thought she saw some dark silhouette moving more quietly beyond one of the few grimy, rain-stained windows that were still intact, but perhaps that was just the product of her imagination. She waited a moment longer. No-one came out or made any other attempt to answer her summons.

Well, she thought. Perhaps that summons was good enough on its own, and that now he knew he had been discovered, the tramp or whomever would simply decide to move on.

Then she heard a footstep inside the building. Another. Another.

Someone was coming out of the shed.

She began to regret that she had ever spoken out in the first place, but counselled herself to remain calm and in command.

A man came out into the dusky light of the dying day.

'*You!*' Annie said angrily.

David O'Neal only smiled easily and reached up to brush his short brown hair back from his forehead. He looked as tall and slim as he had the previous evening, although today his immaculate black suit was smudged and powered with dust following his illicit exploration of the out-buildings. 'Ah, Annabel Tyler,' he said sardonically. 'I thought I recognised your dulcet tones.'

'What are you doing here?' she challenged. 'This is private property.'

He considered for a moment before replying. 'Actually,' he replied after a moment, 'I'm saving you a chore.'

'Oh?'

'Hmm. There's no need for you to go searching through any of the junk in there, hoping to turn up a couple of priceless antiques that'll settle all your boyfriend's debts for him,' he said, indicating the shed behind him by hooking one thumb over his shoulder.

'There aren't any, just a stack of third-rate paintings and pencil-sketches, some old bric-a-brac and about a quarter of a million spiders.'

'I told you last night that I didn't expect to see you again,' she said coolly. 'Winterhaven is not for sale. Andrew Logan's debts will be settled very soon now. And Donald Logan is *not* my boyfriend.'

He arched one eyebrow. 'Really? You could have fooled *me*.'

'You're on private property,' Annie reminded him again. 'And I'm asking you politely to leave. If you don't, I'll call the police.'

'Look, can't we be reasonable over this?' he asked urbanely. 'Your boyfriend — beg pardon, *client* — is in financial difficulty. Glengage is offering him a way out; to sell the estate. We'll pay him the right price, I can assure you. And you could make *yourself* some money, too, if you help us.'

Mention of Glengage made her think about the company again. Sports and leisure facilities. *Sports and leisure facilities*. Where was the connection? She struggled swiftly to find it. She wanted to say something that would shock some of the self-satisfied superiority out of him. But *what*?

And then, in a sudden flash of insight, she thought she understood why he and his precious company were so interested in Winterhaven.

'I'm not interested in your money,' she said. 'And neither is Donald Logan. And I can tell you one more thing with absolute certainty, Mr. O'Neal. The day will never dawn when either Donald or I will allow you to turn Winterhaven into some glorified theme-park!'

She could not have wiped that smug smile off his face any better than if she had stepped forward and slapped him. He stood there stunned. He turned pale. Then something came down over his eyes like a curtain, making them unreadable.

'Who told you that?' he barked furiously. 'That is highly confidential information!'

'It doesn't matter how I found out,' she replied, secretly pleased that she had guessed correctly. 'And in any case, it hardly matters who knows about it and who doesn't, since nothing is going to come of it — at least not on *this* estate.'

His eyes were hooded now, hooded and cunning. 'All right,' he said, making a supreme effort to calm down. 'All right,' he repeated again. 'So, you're a very clever girl. I can appreciate that. Perhaps I underestimated you. Perhaps you want something *more* for helping us. A percentage of the profits when this place opens under the Glengage banner, perhaps?'

'I think you had better go,' she said.

'But just think about what I'm *offering* you,' he said. 'As it stands, this place is nothing but a mausoleum! What we're proposing is to turn it into a gold mine! And I'm offering you a cut of all that!'

'And what would I have to do to earn it? Convince Donald that he should sell out whether he wants to or not? Just so you and your board of directors can grow rich by turning this beautiful, unspoiled estate into some glorified tourist attraction? No, Mr O'Neal. I don't think so!'

He finally understood then that he wasn't going to talk her around. 'You'll be sorry for this,' he predicted grimly. 'It might not happen right away. But sometime soon, when you really stop and think about what you could have had, you'll be sorry you allowed your high-minded principles to get in the way. Only by then, it'll be too late.'

And brushing himself down, he turned on his heel and stalked off across the field, towards the lane where he had presumably parked his car.

Annie let her breath out in a shuddery sigh. Her encounter with him left her feeling shaky. But at least now she thought she had impressed upon him the futility of his continuing to vie for the estate.

Still, if she was honest with herself,

she was no nearer to finding a way of helping Donald solve his financial problems, and with the bank demanding to see him in just two days' time, she knew she must come up with something very, very soon.

Darkness was beginning to stretch across the Highlands as she turned and continued on her way towards the estate. Night-birds began calling to each other high up in the branches of the trees that formed the wild, entangled thicket to the side of the great house.

At last Annie reached the front of the property, climbed the steps and worked the bell-pull, wondering where the day had gone to. Again, so much had happened to her that she was exhausted by it all. She worked the bell-pull again, but still received no response. Perhaps Donald had gone out somewhere — she herself had been away so long, it was possible that he might have gone out to discover what had become of her.

She let herself into the house and called his name. *Donald* echoed up through the vast, empty confines of the house, but she received no response.

Unbuttoning her coat, she decided to go up to her room and change out of her now-muddy clothes, and traipsed tiredly up the wide staircase, still wondering what had become of Donald.

Entering her room, she shrugged out of her jacket and began to unbutton her blouse. Stifling a yawn, she went across to the window, intending to look down upon the beautiful gardens below. She saw Donald then, standing out there on the rugged, grassy banks of the loch, hands plunged into the pockets of his jacket, shoulders hunched against the chill, just watching the patterns of the faintly-blued moon above as it shone down upon the calm, rippled surface of the water.

Oh, Donald . . . she thought.

She wondered what thoughts were running through his mind in that moment. Was he thinking about his grandfather, reliving his grandfather's horrible death out on that seemingly placid loch? Or — and here she felt a faint, eager flutter in her tummy — was he thinking about *her*, fighting to overcome his reluctance to love, to convince himself that happiness *could* be theirs?

Annie hurried back down through the dark house and out across the gardens to the loch. When he heard her coming, Donald turned quickly and almost ran towards her. 'Annie, where the devil have you been? I was just about to come and look for you! I thought . . . well, never mind what I thought. So long as you're safe . . . '

His obvious concern secretly pleased her, and when he came to tower over her, she said, 'I . . . I got lost, that's all. But, Donald . . . '

Taking her by the arm, he turned her back towards the house. 'Come on, let's get you inside. You must be half-frozen — '

'Donald,' she said, a little firmer. 'I know all about the legend of the loch.'

He slowed to a halt and turned to face her again, absently reaching out to turn her collar up against the cold breeze, his handsome face a grim, silent mask.

'But that's all it is, you know,' she went on in a gentler tone. 'Only a legend.'

'That's what you think, is it?' he murmured.

'That's what I *know.*'

He started walking again, slowly, not looking at her. 'If you'd been brought up here, seen the unhappiness that we've seen, you might think differently.'

Impulsively she reached out to lace her arm through his, and asked almost in a whisper, 'Is that . . . is that why you're afraid to commit yourself? Afraid to . . . love?'

He made no immediate response. But then, reluctantly, he nodded. 'That,' he agreed, 'and the fact that I have nothing to offer you. I'm a failure,

Annie. That's the bitter truth of the matter, and coming back to Winterhaven has really brought that fact home to me.'

'That's nonsense, Donald!'

'Is it? I failed in my writing. And when my grandfather really needed me, I wasn't here, so I failed him, too. And now it seems I've even failed you.' He shook his head slowly. 'You deserve better than that, my girl. And one day you'll *find* better.'

'I think I've already found it,' she said quietly.

His short, bitter laugh was a defeated sound. 'No,' he said. 'This is one time that the curse of Winterhaven *isn't* going to work its evil. I'm not going to give it the *chance* to work.'

The silence that came down over them then was a sad, enervating thing. Feeling wretched because of the stubborn determination of his attitude, Annie said, 'What can I do to show you that this curse of yours is nothing but superstition? That it can be overcome?'

163

'It can't,' he replied simply.

'I'll *prove* it to you,' she said with quiet resolution. 'You just see if I don't.'

'How?' he asked.

But she had no answer to that . . . not yet.

7

She tossed and turned restlessly that night, but eventually sleep claimed her, and when the first dim grey streaks of dawn began to daub the sky beyond the window next morning, she rose, slipped into her dressing-gown and hurried to the bathroom, where she washed and applied make-up before returning to her room to dress.

The day had started cold and dreary, so she chose a sensible plaid skirt and a thick, autumnal-brown polo-neck sweater. She went downstairs and into the kitchen at the back of the house. Donald was already pouring coffee for her, hollow-eyed himself following a troubled, sleepless night.

'So,' he said, trying to sound optimistic. 'What have you got planned for today?'

'I want to take a look around Cairn

Cawdor,' she replied vaguely. 'Get some background on your grandfather, find out exactly what kind of man he was, what *he* might have done to save Winterhaven had he been . . . '

' . . . of sound mind?' Donald asked, raising one eyebrow cynically.

She waved aside the offer of some breakfast. 'You're not making this any easier for me, you know,' she censured.

His eyes left her face. 'I'm sorry,' he apologised. 'I'd come in with you, lend a hand, but I've been trying to go through grandfather's papers, see what I can uncover there.'

'That's all right. I don't properly know what I'm looking for myself, yet.'

He fixed her with a very serious look that made her skin tingle pleasantly. 'Maybe we should wish each other luck, then.'

'I do, to you.'

'And I do to you, too.'

'Then between us, how can we fail?'

★　★　★

At half-past eight, she went out into the hallway and dialled Tommy Roberts' number, to request a lift into the village.

Tommy was already waiting for her in his old Hillman Minx by the time she reached the gates. 'The village, is it?'

'Yes, please.'

The countryside flashed by. A light rain was in the air. It pattered against her window and slid down along the glass, propelled by the modest slip-stream.

She asked him to drop her in the high street. As she left the car, she went to pay him but he said, 'Nah. On the house today.'

'Oh really — '

'Go on, put your money away. Just come an' knock for me when you want me to run you back out to Winter-haven.'

She saw that there would be no arguing with him and said, 'All right, Tommy. Thanks.'

It was still relatively early, but already

Cairn Cawdor was beginning to stir. For a moment, Annie stood on the pavement, unsure exactly where to start first. On impulse, she stopped a young woman pushing a baby in a pram and asked for directions to the churchyard. Half a minute later she was turning left into a side street and heading towards the spire she should see on the far side of a neat row of tiny grey-stone houses. Rain was still in the air, but the cool wind seemed to be holding it off.

She didn't really know what had brought her here. Perhaps she was hoping for divine inspiration.

The church turned out to be a beautiful old building set amid neatly-tended grounds. She entered through large, wrought-iron gates and paused a moment to study her surroundings. Away to her left she saw row upon row of headstones, crosses and stone cherubs and angels, the sea of grey monuments punctuated here and there by colorful displays of flowers. The churchyard was peaceful and serene.

Birds chirruped cheerfully in the trees bordering the necropolis. Some of the tranquillity communicated itself to her, and she finally knew some of the peace of mind which had for so long escaped her.

She set out, then, in search of Andrew Logan's grave. She found it fifteen minutes later, and stood there for a long time, reading and re-reading the simple inscription carved upon the recently-installed headstone.

Help me, she asked silently. *Help me to help your grandson. Please, let me break this curse once and for all. Help me to save your estate.*

But no answers came to her, and she left as desperate and hopeless as when she had first arrived.

Next she decided to visit the offices of the local newspaper. She left the churchyard with a purposeful stride, and finding her way back to the high street, stopped another passer-by in order to get further directions.

The newspaper that served Cairn

Cawdor and the surrounding area was situated at the far end of the village, but it was only the matter of a few minutes' brisk walk before she reached her destination.

A helpful receptionist referred her to the head clerk, and once she explained who she was and what she wanted, the head clerk took her along to the chief librarian. The office was large and dusty and the walls were lost behind floor-to-ceiling shelves that were crammed tight with dog-earned manila folders.

The chief librarian turned out to be a matronly woman with very clean skin and steel-grey hair gathered up into a very efficient bun. She listened to Annie's request and then told her to sit herself down at one of the tables in the far corner while she went away to fetch the appropriate file.

A few minutes later the matronly woman returned and set down a thickish folder. She said, 'This is all we have on Andrew Logan, but it goes back twenty years. The earliest material is at the bottom and the most recent is right at the top.'

'Thank you very much,' Annie said sincerely.

Left alone, she opened the folder with a sense of anticipation. As she had expected, the most recent clipping dealt with Andrew's funeral. Beneath that she found the article in which the local paper had broken the news of his death by drowning. Much of what followed was really just a résumé of Andrew Logan's life. Plans to turn Winterhaven into a conference centre were announced. Andrew's reputation as a once-shrewd businessman was confirmed.

Then she came across something interesting — a reference to Andrew and a woman named Eileen Marshall, who had evidently been spending so much time up at the magnificent estate that the paper referred to her as the new lady of Winterhaven.

Eileen Marshall. The name rang a bell with Annie, though she could not immediately think why. Excited now, for she felt that she was starting to make some headway, she continued to read through the clippings, working backwards.

Eileen Marshall had obviously been the woman with whom Andrew had enjoyed a brief period of happiness following his decision to retire from business fifteen years before. Eileen had been an artist of considerable repute. That was where Annie had heard of her — the Tate had held a retrospective of her work not so very long after her death at the age of fifty-six. Though she had failed to achieve critical and popular success in her lifetime, however, her death had stimulated fresh interest in her work, and now she was considered to be one of the country's greatest female painters.

One of the country's greatest paint-ers . . .

She ran her hazel eyes along the line again, not knowing for certain what she was hoping to find buried within it, but knowing that there was *something*. After a moment she sat back, still struggling to dredge up some half-forgotten memory, a memory stirred back to life by that line . . .

And then she thought she had it, and the revelation, the discovery of it, made her feel dizzy, for if she was right, then she felt that she might finally have stumbled across a way of saving Winterhaven.

Her vision misted briefly, but she quickly rubbed away her tears. She wasn't certain yet, must not build up her hopes. But . . .

She closed the folder and returned it to the chief librarian, who asked her if the information it contained had been of any use.

'Possibly,' she replied with a nod. 'Yes — I really think it *has* been.'

She left the offices of the local newspaper in a hurry and made her way back to Tommy Roberts' house, almost unable to control the nervous, anticipatory flutter in her tummy.

Tommy was surprised to see her so soon, but detected something of her animation and, sensing that something momentous was in the offing, drove her swiftly back along the quiet country lane towards Winterhaven, where he dropped her right before the steps leading up to the great oak door.

She thanked him, climbed out of the car and watched him drive away. Then she hurried up the steps, let herself inside and called Donald's name.

He came out of the sitting room wearing a frown. 'Annie? Is everything all right?'

Buoyed up by her news, she nodded, shook her head and shrugged all at once. 'I don't know . . . I think . . . '

'Calm down, now,' he said.

'Wait a moment,' she said breathlessly. 'Just listen to me.' She paused to gather her thoughts. 'Donald, if I could do something to save Winterhaven . . . if I could enable you to complete the conference centre that your grandfather started . . . ' She looked him straight in the eye. 'Would all that prove to you that the curse could be overcome?'

Frowning, he said in an undertone, 'What are you telling me, girl?'

'I think I've found a way to save Winterhaven.'

At once he was attentive. A taut, expectant silence settled between them. He licked his lips nervously and said cautiously, 'Go on, then.'

'Your grandfather,' she explained. 'The woman he met and fell in love with after he retired fifteen years ago, she was Eileen Marshall, the artist.'

He nodded. 'That's right. She was a wonderful artist. A wonderful person. My grandfather was very much in love with her.'

'She lived here for a while, didn't she?'

'Yes.'

'And worked here? Painted here?'

He clearly was not following her. 'Why, yes. She was always painting and sketching.'

'And when she died . . . did she leave

any of her work here?'

At last be began to see the light. 'Yes,' he whispered. 'Yes, she did. She left everything to my grandfather in her will. Paintings, pencil-sketches . . . after she died, grandfather had everything stored away — '

' — in one of the out-buildings just on the far side of the hedgerow?' she asked.

He was startled that she should know that. He nodded. 'Yes,' he said. 'But before you build your hopes up any higher, they're worthless, Annie. Eileen Marshall was a gifted painter, but she never received the recognition she deserved.'

He had fallen into the same trap as David O'Neal, who had discovered Eileen's paintings and pencil-sketches whilst rummaging in the out-buildings the previous afternoon and dismissed them as 'third-rate'.

'She *did* receive recognition,' Annie replied excitedly. 'But *posthumously*.'

He turned away from her and

considered that. If what she said was true, then the paintings and pencil-sketches stored away out there could be worth a fortune. Salvation for Winter-haven. But . . .

'I couldn't . . . wouldn't . . . sell them, Annie,' he said, turning back to her. 'They meant so much to my grandfather, I could never part with them.'

'I wouldn't expect you to,' she replied. 'But . . . answer me this time, Donald. Would you like to realise your grandfather's dream to turn this place into a conference centre, and open the gardens to the public?'

'Of course I would.'

'And do you think you could actually make it work where your grandfather failed?'

'I . . . I would do the best job I had in me.'

'Then what I'm suggesting is that you have Eileen's paintings and sketches authen-ticated and valued this afternoon, and tomorrow we present them as security to the bank for a further loan — a loan with which you can complete what your grandfather started.'

He looked into her face. Something moved in his azure eyes. 'Do . . . ' He cleared his throat, sifting the possibilities now opening up before him. 'Do you think it could work?' he asked.

'You have two of the best reasons in the world for *making* it work,' she said. 'To prove the true worth of your grandfather's plans, and to make sure that Eileen Marshall's paintings remain in your family.'

He continued to look at her. She could tell that he knew she was right. He came towards her, caught up himself now in the heady excitement of the moment, and his smile chased away most if not all of the worry beneath which he had been pinned, and seeing the transformation in him, knowing that she had finally succeeded in taking some of the weight from his shoulders, she felt herself go a little giddy.

She stepped into his embrace, all

other considerations temporarily forgotten. This was a moment of celebration. It should not and would not be marred by other concerns, at least not for a while.

She felt the warmth of him, enjoyed the safe feeling of being held in his strong arms, looked up into his face, his eyes —

With a start she at last became aware of their closeness, a closeness that was as spiritual as it was physical, and there was no mistaking the depth of love that made his eyes shine. She tilted her face up expectantly and he brought his own down upon it, and what followed was a marvellous, tender, prolonged, passionate embrace, an embrace enlivened by a positive shower of kisses.

Some timeless eternity later they broke apart and she looked up at him. At some stage during those few loving moments, all the barriers he had erected between them had disappeared. Now she held him close, enjoyed the feeling of having him holding *her* close, and smiled at him.

'This is all too good to be true,' he said gently, half to himself. 'To think that we've really got a chance to save Winterhaven . . . I'm afraid that I'm going to wake up at any moment and find out that it was all just a dream.'

'It's not a dream, Donald,' she said, slowly coming back down to earth after having visited a paradise to which his kisses had transported her. 'And I'm going to prove it to you. I'll check the telephone directory and get one of the local art dealers to come and examine Eileen's work.'

'I'll get it all up from the sheds, then,' he said.

The transformation in him was amazing. This was the same Donald with whom she had travelled up from London, the man with whom she had fallen in love, a man so completely removed from the near-tragic figure who had said their love was so futile.

'Oh,' he said awkwardly. 'And about

that meeting with the bank tomorrow . . . '

'Yes?'

'I . . . I'd like you to come with me. For us to handle the presentation together.'

'Are you sure?'

'Annie,' he said, and smiled down at her, 'you're my lucky charm. Of *course* I'm sure! Besides, after the way today's turned out, I don't want to push the Logan luck any further than I have to.'

She considered what he was suggesting, and could see no problem in it. 'Well, if that's the way you want it,' she said. 'I'm about as familiar with the problems you've encountered as anyone.'

'Thank you.'

Then he turned away, grabbed his jacket, let himself out and set off across the field toward the sheds, to begin transporting the paintings and sketches back to the house.

★　★　★

Annie rang an art dealer in the nearest big town and asked if someone might come out to Winterhaven to authenticate and value some pictures, ostensibly for insurance purposes. The man at the other end of the line, who had identified himself as a Mr Hamilton, didn't sound too enthusiastic, and after telling her just how busy he was at the moment, suggested the following Wednesday afternoon.

'Ah. I'm afraid that's a bit too late for my needs at the moment,' she replied.

'Well, I'm sorry, but that's the best I can do,' Mr Hamilton said. 'How many of these paintings have you got, anyway? Perhaps if you were to bring them to the gallery . . . ?'

'Well, I think it's going to be too difficult to transport them. There are around twenty canvases, some of them quite large, and two portfolios filled with pencil-sketches.'

The voice at the other end of the phone began to sound interested. 'Are they signed?' he asked.

'Initialled 'E.M.' and dated, yes.'

'And do you have any idea who the artist is?'

'Yes — Eileen Marshall,' said Annie.

There was a long pause following that. Then the art dealer said, 'Are you *sure? The* Eileen Marshall?'

'Yes, *the* Eileen Marshall. But obviously I would like some expert confirmation.'

'Well, my dear Miss Tyler, that puts an entirely different complexion on the matter. I wonder — might I call round this afternoon at, say, half-past two?'

★ ★ ★

Mr Hamilton was as good as his word, and spent almost two hours going through the collection, which Donald had set up in the sitting room. The art dealer asked them both numerous questions, clarified ownership, consulted several books and catalogues and finally pronounced that there was no doubt in his mind that the works of art spread out before him were definitely by Eileen Marshall.

'And that's not all,' he added. 'Marshall's work is not my specialty by any means, but I would say that what you have assembled here is some of her very best work.'

'You can authenticate them for us, then?' prodded Donald. 'And estimate their present value?'

'Of course,' Hamilton responded. And after making what appeared to be some extensive and complicated calculations, he finally scribbled a rough figure down onto a piece of paper and passed it over to him. The number was long, and had an apparently endless procession of noughts and commas in it.

Donald had trouble accepting the evidence of his eyes. 'Don't think I'm calling your expertise into question, Mr Hamilton,' he said in awe. 'But surely, this can't be right?'

Hamilton chuckled as he reached for his overcoat and hat. 'I think you'll find that it *is*, Mr Logan. And given the enormity of the sum, the sooner you get these paintings insured, the better.'

8

The letter Donald had received from the bank made it clear in no uncertain terms that its board of directors wanted to see him at two o'clock on Friday afternoon. That in itself presented no great problem, but it did mean that both he and Annie had to endure a seemingly endless morning just waiting for the time of their appointment to arrive.

Up in her room, Annie checked her reflection one last time before they started out. She was wearing the same efficient-looking black suit she had worn only a week earlier, when she had first been given the responsibility of trying to save Winterhaven from its creditors. And what a week that had turned out to be, she now reminded herself ruefully.

She straightened the collar of her

snow-white blouse, brushed imaginary dust from her lapels and lastly checked her hair and make-up, knowing that it was crucial that she make the right impression. Then, at last, she grabbed her bag and went downstairs.

Donald, himself dressed smartly in a pale grey suit cut in casual lines, a white shirt and maroon tie, was waiting for her at the foot of the stairs. As he watched her descend the staircase, his eyes filled with admiration.

'You're ready to go, then?' he asked.

'To quote the well-worn cliché,' she replied, 'as ready as I'll ever be.'

As they left the house, he said softly, 'Thank you.'

She frowned. 'What for?'

'For giving me hope.'

'Then you believe me? When I tell you that the legend is just that?'

He glanced uncertainly around the house. 'Ask me that again after the bank's said yes.'

They met Tommy Roberts at the gates, as Donald had arranged the night before, and allowed him to ferry them through Cairn Cawdor and on towards the town of Ayrling where, by coincidence, Mr Hamilton had his art gallery.

'Important meeting, is it, Donald?' Tommy asked over his shoulder. 'I mean, you look right posh today, the pair of you, all done up like that.'

'I assume that was meant as a compliment,' teased Annie, smiling affectionately at him.

'It was, love, it *was*.'

'Well, you're right,' said Donald. 'In fact, it couldn't be *more* important.'

'To do with Winterhaven, is it?'

'Yes.'

'Then I wish you all the luck, mate. Want me to hang around for you? Save you having to find a cab to bring you back later.'

'Well, it might take a while.'

'I've got nothing better to do.'

'Thanks, then,' Donald replied. 'You never know, if it all goes wrong we might be in need of a friendly face.'

They arrived in Ayrling about twenty

minutes before the appointment, and killed time just window-shopping. Then, finally, they made their way to the bank, introduced themselves and were told to wait in a comfortable ante-room until summoned.

A further ten minutes passed before a secretary came out and told them that the bank's directors were ready to see them. As they rose, Donald caught Annie's eye and murmured, 'All or nothing, eh?'

She nodded. 'All or nothing.'

They went through into a plush office, where they were asked to take seats before a group of four austere-looking men.

What followed was a detailed discussion about the state of Winterhaven's finances, and the bank's concern for the money it had already advanced in respect of Andrew Logan's proposed conference centre. Between them, Donald and Annie fielded the questions as best they could and argued the case for giving Donald more time in which to get the project back on track.

'I am afraid we have come to the stage where we have run *out* of time,' one of the men told her candidly. 'I — that is, *we* — agree that Andrew Logan's plans were impressive, and we believe that, had he handled his finances better, he could have turned Winterhaven into a very profitable concern. But he did *not* handle his finances as we would have liked. Therefore we have no choice but to foreclose on the property.'

'I can and *will* turn the Winterhaven Conference Centre into a going concern,' Donald argued with sudden passion. 'But I need a little more time, and an extension on my credit.'

One of the men seated behind the long mahogany table actually snorted. 'An extension on your credit?' he echoed. 'Mr Logan, your grandfather practically signed away his entire estate to us in order to raise money for his project, and when he died he had nothing, absolutely *nothing*, to show for it. How can we extend more money with a track record like that?' His rheumy eyes found those of Donald and he demanded, 'What more collateral could you possibly offer?'

Donald paused for just a moment, then sat a little straighter, squared his shoulders almost imperceptibly, and said confidently, 'Tell them, Annie.'

She did, and took the greatest of pleasure in so doing. 'Twenty oil paintings and one hundred and sixty five pencil-sketches by the artist Eileen Marshall,' she announced, taking Hamilton's valuation from her bag and passing it across for the directors to examine. 'As you will see, we've already had the paintings authenticated and valued, but you are more than welcome to seek an independent opinion.'

She felt a surge of excitement as she watched the four bankers read the valuation. If their raised eyebrows were any indication, the worth of the paintings on the open market clearly astounded them.

Throwing her a wink, Donald added, 'I could be wrong, but I don't think you will find more solid collateral anywhere, gentlemen.'

After a moment's muttered discussion, the directors asked them to wait outside while they considered the matter further. A quarter of an hour later they were called back into the office where, with a sober face, the bankers' spokesman announced their decision.

★   ★   ★

Later, as Tommy drove them back in the direction of Cairn Cawdor, the early darkness began to fall like fine grey sand to form dusk, and a low mist started to rise off the ground, making driving difficult and slow.

'I dunno,' Tommy said, leaning forward over the steering wheel in order to see better out through the windscreen. 'Rest of the year we're lucky for the weather, have it pretty mild considerin', but every autumn we get these perishin' mists.'

At last they reached and passed through Cairn Cawdor. Half an hour later they began to approach the gates of Winterhaven. 'Right,' said Tommy. 'Here we are.'

He slowed to a stop and they got out. 'Thanks, Tommy,' said Donald, paying the fare and clapping the older man affectionately on one shoulder. 'See you.'

He and Annie stood side by side in the wreathing fog until the Bogus Scotsman turned the car around and set off back to Cairn Cawdor, and as she watched him go, it suddenly occurred to Annie that she was going to miss him when she returned to London, just as she would miss these beautiful wilds, the friendliness of the villagers, the village itself, and of course, Donald and Winterhaven.

For the sad but simple truth was that she *would* be returning to London. And why stay? She had been hoping that Donald would finally find the courage to dismiss his misgivings and commit himself once and for all where their future was concerned, but he hadn't. Maybe, in the final analysis, he simply hadn't been *able* to. Or maybe the curse had too powerful a hold on him after all.

Either way, she had willed him to say something to her after they left the bank, to give her some sign or indication of his intentions, but he had lapsed into a thoughtful silence and, it seemed to her, he had deliberately avoided the issue. And so she had decided, on the journey back to Winterhaven, that all she could do now was take her leave on the morrow and hope that the shock of it would make him realise what he stood to lose, what the curse would really *cost* him if he let her go.

And if that didn't work, then she would leave his life as quickly as she had entered it, and vice versa — and that was a prospect she could hardly bear to consider.

Donald, unaware of the direction her thoughts had taken, took her by the arm and began to lead her up the gravel drive towards the house, but she held back, and he frowned. 'Are you okay?' he asked.

'Are *you?*' she countered.

He ran one hand up through his hair. 'I guess. Got a lot to think about, I suppose.'

'Me, too,' she replied. 'I suppose.' Then, as words failed her, she sighed. 'You go on ahead. I just want to be on my own for a while.'

He studied her more closely. 'Out *here?*' he asked. 'In *this?*'

'Yes.'

'Are you *sure* you're all right?'

'Yes. Really.'

He hesitated a moment longer, then said, more for something to say than anything else, 'I'll get the fire going in the drawing room, then.'

She watched him fade into the fog

and tried to shrug off the feeling that all this was coming to an end, but it wasn't easy. She had hoped that things might have worked out differently today, but they hadn't. He still seemed so hesitant to say what was really in his heart, and had chosen instead to say nothing.

She shivered, and told herself that Donald had been right. It was no night to be outside, thinking such demoralising thoughts.

With a shiver, she started up the drive towards the house, her footsteps crunching through the early darkness, the sound faintly muffled by the mist.

She hadn't gone very far when she heard a soft sound behind her that made her turn.

Although she strained to pierce the shifting grey curtain, she couldn't see a thing. And yet . . .

What was that?

No . . . no. She dismissed the notion, and carried on walking. *And yet*, she thought, *it sounded just like someone calling my name.*

She continued on her way up the drive, determined not to give in to the urge to hurry or perhaps even break into a run. Instead she kept walking, her back straight, her shoulders squared, droplets of mist bursting against her cheeks, chilling her already-chilled skin.

And then —

' . . . *Annniiieeee* . . . '

She stopped again and spun around quickly, hoping to surprise whomever it was. Only mist swirled before her eyes. But there could be no mistaking it this time — someone had *definitely* called her name. Donald? No. No, by this time, she knew Donald's voice as well as she knew her own. Then who — ?

Warily she opened her mouth, licked her lips, cleared her throat and said, 'Who . . . who's there?'

Silence was her only reply. Silence . . . and then . . .

' . . . *Annniiieee* . . . '

Now her hazel eyes were everywhere at once, and as hard as she tried to fight it, she felt her fear rising. 'Who's there?'

Nothing.

She turned and carried on walking, faster now, faster . . .

A shiver ran through the bushes at the side of the drive.

' . . . *Annniiieee* . . . '

Faster, faster . . .

And then, all at once, she heard another sound, the crunching of gravel, footfalls that were not her own. In that same instant she sensed that she was no longer alone, and was just about to turn again when —

— when someone reached out and grabbed her arm.

'Uh!'

'Good evening, Miss Tyler.'

Surprise washed her face of every other emotion. '*You!*' she cried.

David O'Neal gave a throaty chuckle. 'I really had you going then, didn't I?'

Angrily she shrugged out of his hold. 'How dare you!' she said with feeling. 'That was a stupid, irresponsible thing to do . . . but no more than I would have expected from you!'

He sobered. 'Now, now,' he said in mock reproof. 'Is that any way to treat a fellow who's spent most of the afternoon stuck here, waiting for you to get back from your date?'

'Waiting for *me?*'

'I wanted to see if you'd changed your mind about helping us to buy Winterhaven.'

'Winterhaven is *not* for sale. I've already told you that.'

He made a gesture of impatience. 'Look, let's not beat around the bush. You know as well as I do that the bank — '

'The bank,' said a new voice, cutting through the fog, 'has just agreed to extend me all the credit I need to finish converting Winterhaven into a conference centre.'

They both spun then, Annie feeling almost faint with relief, as Donald strode back through the fog towards them. Beside her, David O'Neal took an involuntary pace backward and said, '*What?*'

'You heard me,' Donald replied, his voice deep and authoritative. 'Now, I don't know who you are and I don't know what business you *think* you have with Miss Tyler, here. But I *do* know that you're trespassing, and that if you don't get off my property within the next ten seconds I'm going to call the police — or throw you out of here myself.'

Blustering, O'Neal said, 'You're lying. About the bank, I mean. You're finished, Logan. Everyone knows that.'

'Then maybe you can do me a favour,' said Donald, his voice suddenly sounding dangerously reasonable. 'You can start spreading the word that, far from being *finished*, as you put it, the Logans of Winterhaven are here to *stay.*'

'Going to buck the curse, are you?' O'Neal sneered.

Donald came closer and put one arm around Annie's shoulders. 'Yes,' he replied. 'I'm going to 'buck the curse'. And shall I tell you why? Because Annie

200

here told me that I wasn't the failure I thought I was, and over the past few days I've come to see that she was right. Because she told me she was going to save this estate when all the odds were stacked against it, and she was right about *that*, too. So what can I do when she tells me I've been a fool to believe in the curse? With her kind of track record, I have to believe her about *that* as well, don't I?'

She felt the gentle pressure of his arm across her back and shoulders in a comforting, loving squeeze. 'Now,' he continued, 'I think you'd better leave. And if you know what's good for you, you'll never come anywhere near Annie, or Winterhaven, ever again. Do ye *ken?*'

O'Neal muttered something dark, but he wouldn't look Donald in the eye, and slowly he started backing away into the mist, doubtless to return to wherever he had parked his Porsche.

'Drive carefully,' Annie told him sweetly as he finally vanished from sight.

A few moments later they heard the growl of his car engine and listened in silence as he drove away.

Donald turned to her then, and holding her by the elbows, said, 'I *have* been a fool, haven't I?'

'Yes,' she replied honestly. 'I thought . . . after we left the bank, you were so quiet . . . '

'I was thinking,' he said. 'Trying to find the right words to express just how much you mean to me, and how grateful I am for everything that you've done here.'

'And have you found any?'

'I think so,' he replied. 'But first, wee lassie, I think it's only fair to tell you that, as perfect as you are, you don't get *everything* right.'

'Oh?'

'Well, yesterday you told me I had two reasons to make a go of things here,' he explained. 'To prove the true worth of my grandfather's plans, and to make sure that Eileen Marshall's paintings remained in the family.'

'What's wrong with that?'

'Nothing. But you left out the most important reasons of all.'

'Which are . . . ?'

'My wife and children,' he replied, adding quickly, 'That is, assuming you *want* children? Eventually, I mean.'

She arched one eyebrow at him. 'Are you by any chance *proposing* to me, Donald Logan?' she breathed.

He smiled. 'Do you know, Annabel Tyler, I *do* believe I *am*.'

Tears welled in her eyes. 'Oh, Donald . . . '

Tentatively he asked, 'Does that mean you will? So that we can spend the rest of our lives together, making a go of this place, raising our children here, proving once and for all that love can and *will* flourish at Winterhaven?'

For a moment she was unable to speak. Then, as tears coursed down her cheeks and she went into his arms, she nodded emphatically and husked, 'Yes, Donald. That's *exactly* what it means . . . '

Without warning then, he picked her up and spun her around, and for a moment the two of them went a little crazy there in the misty lane, until at length he set her back down, and arm in arm they crunched back up the drive, hugging and giggling like teenagers, until nothing was left in the misty drive save the echoes of their voices, already making plans for the future . . . that and the cheerful, welcoming lights of Winterhaven.

THE END

We do hope that you have enjoyed reading this large print book.

Did you know that all of our titles are available for purchase?

We publish a wide range of high quality large print books including:
Romances, Mysteries, Classics General Fiction Non Fiction and Westerns

Special interest titles available in large print are:
The Little Oxford Dictionary Music Book, Song Book Hymn Book, Service Book

Also available from us courtesy of Oxford University Press:
Young Readers' Dictionary (large print edition) Young Readers' Thesaurus (large print edition)

For further information or a free brochure, please contact us at:
**Ulverscroft Large Print Books Ltd., The Green, Bradgate Road, Anstey, Leicester, LE7 7FU, England.
Tel:** (00 44) **0116 236 4325
Fax:** (00 44) **0116 234 0205**

Other titles in the
Linford Romance Library:

DARK MOON

Catriona McCuaig

When her aunt dies, Jemima is offered a home with her stern uncle, but vows to make her own way in the world by working at a coaching inn. She falls for the handsome and fascinating Giles Morton, but he has a menacing secret that could endanger them both. When Jemima is forced to choose between her own safety and saving the man she loves, she doesn't hesitate for a moment — but will they both come out of it alive?

HOME IS WHERE THE HEART IS

Chrissie Loveday

Jayne and Dan Pearson have moved to their dream house . . . a huge dilapidated heap on top of a Cornish cliff. The stresses of city life are behind them, their children consider their new home 'the coolest house ever', and the family's future looks rosy. But when a serious accident forces them to re-think their dream, they embark upon a completely different way of life — though its pleasures and disasters bring a whole new meaning to the word *stress* . . .

A HATFUL OF DREAMS

Roberta Grieve

Sally Williams works in a milliner's salon, but her ambition is to own her own shop. When she delivers a hat to Lady Isabelle Lazenby, she becomes flustered by Lady Isabelle's handsome cousin, Charles Carey — but finds herself attracted to the footman, Harry. However, Charles' interest in Sally causes a rift in her friendship with Harry, who also seems to be close with Maggie, Lady Isabelle's maid. Will Sally achieve her ambition? And could there be a future for Sally and Harry?